CW01219866

Printed in the United States of America.
For information, contact www.daystarbooks.com

DayStarBooks

www.daystarbooks.com

Acknowledgment

I owe a dept of gratitude to my wife, who restrained from displaying even a small hint of restlessness, patiently waited for years, and not chastised my squandering of time.

Prologue

As a kid I spent an enormous amount of time down by the river, being drawn like a magnet to the long stretch of concrete docks, I would remain there all day under the pretense that I was fishing. I would walk the shores for miles, moving from one spot to the next. *I later discovered that the sky above this river was alive.* I developed a special relationship with the cloud host of beings. I would slowly come to understand they were the reason my thirdEye was modified to see a hidden reality.

I observed that our earth, moon and its inhabitants are much more sinister than what we have been taught. With what old folks call a thirdEye, I will reveal a truth concealed from human eyesight.

As a child, I observed a silent intruder standing in our home. He did not enter by doors and all the windows were locked.

Many people have described a weird sleep paralysis after falling asleep. Suddenly awaken, heart pounding, terrified, unable to move even a finger or cry out for help. During this time they sense the presents of someone else standing in a dark corner of the room.

The medical profession missed-diagnosed this phenomenon is caused by poor blood circulation—nothing could be further from the truth. What people are really experiencing is the presence of an invisible life form. My brothers and I have named this intruder the “stuck thang” or "boogieman". The truth behind my childhood fear was and still is very real. I have nSopia-a rare continuous opened third eye. I have observed these nocturnal beings for over fifty years. They sought to destroy my own third eye as they have done to so many others. I managed to evade detection by not reacting to their invisible presence and pretending to not see them at all. I have observed what they do to you in the dark.

The fact is, parts of man’s mental thoughts are harvested every night. We are visited, immobilized, and maliciously taunted by our captors every night. You sometimes accidentally awake in the middle of this malevolent process.

This book will set you on a quest to discover who these nocturnal beings are. I will expose you to a night filled with things hidden from your own two eyes.

All cultures have recorded this strange nightly experience. Children of today have tried to express this weird occurrence.

With great trepidation, I tell this story.
But, no matter what unfolds after you read my accounts, if you are startled awake from sleep, mysteriously paralyzed with an invisible hostile being standing at your bedside...

…with urgency I say...
"Remember the DayStar".

The River's Sky was revealed to me for a reason. Over several decades, I learned the mystery of my linkage to this sky.

For me, the past fifty years of my life has been a very strange journey. Not involved with physical travel of great distance, as it has been one arduous, incremental self-awareness process. It seemed at times to require unbearable discipline, exhaustive patience and intolerable tolerance. During this gradual unveiling of my true identity, many times I thought something was wrong with my life. Time has revealed the truth.

Mankind and the sinister celestial inhabitants of the earths other hidden five moons are about to be exposed. This is not without risk to all who read these words.

But, it is time… ThirdEye reality has arrived.

Chapter 1

Of all the unseen things, one of the first I found to be most astonishing. Earth has six populated moons. The one seen with the naked eye is the smallest of the cluster. The other five moons are invisible to human sight. These moons are heavily populated by horrendous nocturnal beings. At night, they descend to earth in mass by the millions.

For the past 50 years I have lived a
secret life known to no one. I have lived life here and at the
same time witness life through the eye's of a
civilization known as the Son's of Te-naka-to-non.
I have seen the Tenakatonon, I have seen the Mac-at-a.
I have seen the Boogiemen.

What I have kept secret, in-a-hurry
I now write.

For…

The mMutota are coming!

A story based on some true events, and may affect your night the day you read it.

Through the eyes of the beings who reside in the forefront on the river of man, I sometimes see catastrophic events that might affect those of us further back down the river of life. It is for this cause that they reveal to me what their own eyes behold.

Some people can see more of the reality that surrounds them. They can perceive a multiple realities. They sometimes observe manlike creatures moving sinisterly among us as we prepare for bed or lay asleep. If you are one of these thireEye persons, you are one of the few remaining who poses a very real threat to proving the existence of the boogieman.

When I say true, I mean… aclasstru (the things I speak of are real) whether you can see it or not!

If you see only what the physical eye perceives, you are blind to ninety-nine other realities.

Chapter 2

The year was nineteen seventy-nine on a calm sunny day. I was standing at the edge of the Detroit River just east of Third Street in an abandoned parking lot. Oddly, I looked up in the sky and I saw the greatest cloud I have ever seen. It stretched from one end of the earth's horizon to the other, not at the height or middle of the sky but offset slightly toward the northeast horizon. The weather was calm and perfect for an end of summer kind of day, a light breeze passed over the open field, brushed lightly across my face, and caused the taller plants and grasses to sway gently back and forth in visual dancing patterns. This was a very calm place, in a way it had become my private sanctuary. It was a place where I would go to clear my mind or relax. Sometime after a rough day at work before going home, I would park just so I could see the river and my nerves would calm. My son was with me on this day and he was just as curious about what I was staring at in the sky. I point up and said "look at that huge funny looking cloud in the sky". As I pointed, he was already looking at this cloud but he was not seeing what I was seeing, I realized he could not see it. I felt something eerie about the cloud, my fatherly instincts kicked in. Something told me, that the less my son knew the less danger he would be in. I placed my son in the car so that he would be out of harms way as he resisted, for he too wanted to be a part of what ever it was that got my attention. This cloud was brighter than normal formations of the cumulonimbus variety and I had the strangest sensation that this cloud was alive. I was struck by the fact that certain large portions of its outer fringes seem too accelerated then decelerate moving independently from the main formation. These portions of clouds would reinsert themselves back into the larger configuration momentarily. This process was repeated all along the fringes of the cloud.

Suddenly a disturbance at the outer fringe of cloud, a small flash of lighting, completely separated a large portion of cloud—my emotions became slightly fearful just as this event occurred. I sensed that this entity was in fact alive! Then it slowly, so as to not cause any further alarm from me as though it detected my fear, it started to descend. It's tumbling and rolling into itself over and over again was almost calming. It continued its slow hypnotic descent, drifting down from the sky. After it reached a height just above my eye level, it started to proceed closer to where I was standing. I begin to see its peculiar shape. A boot made of clouds? "I subconsciously thought". The initial fear I felt at first gave way to curiosity. This was a cloud in the shape of a boot. As I stared, it started moving with an occasional small zigzag as if it was being guided. It continued toward me more ground level now. The cloudy boot made its way across the landscape and stopped at my left leg. The clouds then immediately engulfed my left foot. Strange, very strange I thought. After the boot of clouds fully engulfed my left foot, I began to feel a rush through my body, not of a sick feeling, but as if my body was responding to something old but yet new. I wanted to pull away but I could not do such an insulting thing for I felt that it knew my body better than I knew myself. I started seeing flashes of lights and the sky looked different somehow, I started hearing voices and understanding what I was hearing. For a brief moment I began understanding the secrets of the old and mysterious treasures, thoughts that would not be revealed to me until after my death when all things would be known. I had the knowledge that these beings were part of a great host masquerading as clouds hiding their presents from all other living things. Through my mind's eye, my third eye, I was able to grasp the true span of this mysterious cloud. Its extension was at that time a truly incomprehensible distance, and yet I could not see the distance, but I could feel the great abyss from here to its end. I felt the present of a great person illuminating even further in the expanse—acknowledging my awareness of my seeing them all for the first time. This old and very distant being was ultimately the greatest of the host. At the time of this joining, I was well aware that the entity was in complete control of what we saw and who we saw. For during this encounter I was made to comprehend their vastness of this one legion crossing in this universe, but I would later learn just how awesome their power really was. I could actually see out of my eyes and then, quite frankly, I could see out of eyes I knew not, with the understanding that I was seeing through the eyes of the son's of tanakatonon. Also, I was able to hear my normal physical surroundings and at the same time I heard cosmic preaching. I could not explain how I felt during this encounter only but, that my body did not belong to me for a moment.

With this boot made of clouds…on my left foot, I now hear what they hear. I can see what they see.

What the sons of tanakatonon see, in a hurry I write!

Months passed, then from great distances and in muffled thundering I heard this word...

"magnanimity."

Chapter 3

Months passed and wondering if I would learn more from the earlier episode, but then from great distances, I starting hearing dissertations while I was at work, sitting at the dinner table, sitting by the fireplace, driving, sleeping, fishing, doing something or nothing. I started feeling if I had a medical condition and maybe I should go to the doctor. The first time I heard the distant sermon I was sitting at my desk at work. I worked in an old turn of the century building, with a talkative guard sitting at the front desk, noisy clankity elevators, and squeaking floors, I thought maybe the building was haunted. As an analyst at National Bell I befriended most of the employees working there. My desk was on the third floor of the building and to start our work day we would have a morning group meeting. I hated meetings, I preferred to work continuously through breaks, lunch and meetings. I felt they were unnecessary on a daily basis; it interrupted my workflow momentum. We would review yesterday's achievements and today's goals. Light insults would exchange back and forth between team members. Sometimes the meeting would be great because some my close co-workers would keep me laughing throughout the session. However, I would mostly remain quiet in hopes to expedite a quick closure to the ritual. Mostly, it was an exercise of egos involving just two people, the manager and the top performing YPS, Yellow Pages Sales Rep Vivian Cruso. This test of mental acuity would go on for a third of the meeting until one or both would realize that a capitulation would mean a slight condescending defeat to their opponent. After these office meetings, we would all migrate back to our desks, some standing and pushing their chairs and others like me would return to their cubical by scooting backwards while still sitting in my chair, to begin a normal work routine. On this particular day something very abnormal happened, something that made me sit very still and as my elementary school teacher name Mr. West would say…"give my undivided attention".

This day in particular while in the cubical working away, glancing at notes pasted on the board in front of me, and reviewing the client contact reports I had to enter each morning. Within minutes I went into a trance, I heard someone preaching in a distance, passionately and reverently, it was to say the least very interesting. I thought it was just another mental drift into daydream land. Unknown to me, I was drawn more and more into the speech from an unknown orator, as he became more audible, I could hear him loud and clear now. This did not seem like one of my imaginary drifts. Thinking back, the option to ignore the voice was in fact never an option. The noises of the everyday office unknowingly disappeared into silence. What I heard could have been described as a voice in my mind, a great discourse, a most stirring oration. Chill bumps tingled on both my arms and head as I listened to an invisible person preaching a most stirring sermon, I was spell bound as I heard and understood his magnificent and magnanimous words. I felt weightless and afloat; all of a sudden, I felt no condemnation as I was so moved by the content of his speech. Most of the dialogue contained lessons of social conduct centering around a word that i would never heard of before, magmnti, magagnanimmiaty, magnnanty as I struggled to remember this strange word. I missed-pronounced it in an attempt to not forget it, later I found it in the dictionary it was …"magnanimity", "above resentment and revenge, gracious in forgiveness, he who make sacrifice for worthy ends". Yes, this was the gist of his speech in the greatest sermon I had ever heard since that time.

Over a great distance, I see... Clouds of people stacked high...

As he spoke, I felt a full spectacle of beings. Starting at his location and looking back, I saw light years of listeners. I looked in front, above, and behind me, all of us were held spell-bound by the words being spoken. Chills bumps appeared on my skin. I continued my surveillance of the immense size of the crowd; my peripheral vision was full of people from edge to edge of eyesight, they looked like a wall of people. From the horizon continuing upward into the clear star filled night sky getting smaller as I looked higher, forming a continuous earth size tunnel of spectators. My attention was drawn to a section of the audience in front of my field of view. I could clearly see their great jubilation and excitement. Distance did not diminish the detail of those eyes. I will never forget those bright beautiful "good to see you" smiling eyes as some of their heads slightly tilted downward staring in my direction. I also felt they were waiting in huge anticipation for a signal. On this signal, they would all at once in massive clouds, pour down from the skies to the earth like a thousand years of pent-up flashflood rain waters.

The orator was communicating as though it is common to share the same space with the dead and the living. I have seen with my own newly enhanced eye people who have passed on in the attendance of dissertations.

At one point during this sermon, I felt like shouting—never before had I felt this way when listening to boring sermons at church. There was thunderous applause from the attending audience as the invisible and distant orator continued his speech. The applause was so loud that it broke the universal silence. The great applause, it was followed by immediate silence. He starts to speak again, and again another deafening applause follows, then silence. After a long silence, the listeners could not contain themselves at this point. The audience was such at awe they restrained and held their composure as long as they could. He summarizes his message to the audience and carefully ends his sermon. The over-anxious listeners almost instantly erupt with a deafening and final thunderous ovation of approval that lasted for several minutes.

Yes I have observed him preaching from afar, though I sat there, in an old turn of the century office building at my desk, in a small cubical, on Costman Boulevard.

He talked of morality, eucumene (law of house), archie(the beginning of things and the end of things), he speaks of AgnusDomino(of the great one even greater than the mMutota and son's themselves. We all were held spellbound to the sermons of the famed invisible orator. He speaks to the living sons of tanakatonon – for they are among a few who accepted his criticism, reflect, and make correction.

After returning home, I told my mother about the sermon I heard in my head while sitting at my desk at work. I explained the effect it had on my body, the loud applause from the virtual audience. I described the loud applauses as "the sound that a hand full of wet french-fries make when dropped in hot grease", she inquired a little and concluded that it might be a sign or a calling from God that I should become a preacher. However, this was not a sign. I was a spectator in an audience listening to a stirring oration. As I will later learn, there is a reason to program discretion into the minds of certain men.

I wondered for years if I should tell of these strange sermons I heard and the things I now see with my enhanced eye, but each time I contemplated telling, a strong feeling of restraint would overwhelm me. When I persisted in sharing my experience, a dream would follow and make me aware that I should say nothing. There were times I knew not only my life but also the lives of my immediate family would be threatened by the boogieman–which is very real but invisible to your eyes. I always knew that there was someone else living amongst us, at the time I just did not know who or what they were. Shortly, I would discover who, and just how powerful the "boogiemen" truly was. I would understand the dept of their empires, why they are so feared by all, and the reason they appear in so many legends. I would also discover another secret that even the boogieman wished had remained unknown from the eyes of man.

Someone or something from a far away place was actually guiding me. They would test the words that I choose to come out of my mouth just seconds before I think to speak. They would test and measure by the milliseconds my actions or reaction to instruction. This I found was for my own good, because they, unlike me knew the full power of the boogieman, ruler of earth and the galaxies. One small miss-step or action could mean detection or destruction. However, my distant cloudHost knew the true name and true power of what we simply call the boogieman. The boogieman I discovered is not a myth!

No longer feeling any warnings to remain silent, caution has given place to urgency. The son's, many of them stand close now. I see glimpses of them standing for a split second. Other times, I see them continuously scanning into the ether at a vast distance. Things have unexpectedly changed. I know my time has come to tell what it is I have seen over the past fifty years, those things of the mMutota, of secondMan(we called the boogieman), and of the son's of Tenakatonon.

So this morning is different. This morning, I rise with the purpose, a purpose to warn of another kind of flood, another kind of cloud, whose symbol could be that of a storm. The mMutota are coming.

The arrival of the mMutota into our universe descent-level can best be described as the arrival of many storms.

However, there is a more sinister threat that has occurred on earth for thousands of years. It's concealed in children's fairy tales. While they are young, some children can see vague shadows of the invisible reality that surround them. If they no longer can observe this obscure realm, it is because the boogieman permanently their disabled third eye. Just because we are blind to the full spectrum of reality, does not mean it cease to exist.

Chapter 4

Often when I say boogieman I will mean secondMan or menMateria (the river has divided into three separate branches.) All branches are of the same water.) I will often refer to secondMan as the boogieman as you have come to call him. He is a race of nocturnal beings invisible to human eyes.

My encounter with alternate life forms started years before the boot of clouds incident. My brothers and I would talk about "the stuck thang" as they would call it – “can not move at night thang”, “the boogieman.” We all laugh about the experiences. As night came on one occasion, I asked them, what about the people who cause the stuck thang? My two brothers causally responded that they are not aware of any people. Yeah, there is always a man who comes into the room, this is what causes "the stuck thang", and he immobilized every living thing in his presence as a security measure before he would approach our beds.

As stated earlier, older siblings try to frighten the younger siblings with stories. My two older brothers were no exception. There were stories about yes, and the infamous boogieman. This legendary nocturnal created would appear at night and get you. He would hide under your bed and reach out a grab your ankles if you got out of bed to go to the bathroom in the middle of the night or if you fell asleep with your foot dangling over the edge of your bed. Yeah, I was frightened all right. Right from the first time I heard the story when I was around four or five years old. That is because my boogieman I discovered later in life was much different from the imaginary boogieman my brothers told me about. (My boogieman would occasionally pay me a visit from the darkest shadows in the room. To me my boogieman was very real. I had a great imagination heck, my boogieman even came with special paralyzing force fields he came with what we back then could only describe it as "the stuck-thang").

I thought everyone had the same experiences. I thought we all saw and heard the same things. After going to bed then falling to sleep, I would abruptly awaken. Nothing would happen nor would I see anything. But I would be so afraid to go and get a drink of water or go to the bath room. I would lie there even the thought of just looking around the room was a terrifying thought. So, I would stay hidden under the covers. Oh boy, do not even think about staring into a darker part of the room like a certain corner or a closet because you would certainly see something. There was surely eyes there, staring out at you, and if I stared at him or we locked eyes, then he would surely come across the room and get me. The safest thing to do was to stay under the covers, and suppress my urge to go to the bathroom. I was always hoping that someone else would wake up and go the bathroom. If the boogieman wanted to get someone, he would get one of my big billy-goat brothers first. If nothing happened to them, then it was an all clear signals that it was just my imagination once again and I would make my dash to the toilet and back to my bed as quick as I could.

I was in elementary school in about the fourth or fifth grade, even I knew the boogieman along with Santa Clause was a big fake and just fairy tales for young cowardly kids. Not every night would I be afraid of the dark because really I was kind of fearless and afraid of nothing else. I can recall not even huge barking dogs was I afraid of. Most nights were normal, but some came with this weird boogieman staring out at me from the dark.

To get the experiences out without receiving ridicule from my brothers, I would mask the midnight experiences as a dream. Instead of saying… when I go up the bathroom, I would say… you know, I dreamed I got up to go to the bathroom, and before I went into the bathroom I looked to my left toward the kitchen… and I saw my brother Stan walking very slow with his hands behind his head. When I called to him, he ignored me. He did even look around, with a white T-shirt on and kept on walking, walking… right through the kitchen table! I just watched my own older brother walk right through the kitchen table, right on toward the front door, disappearing into the darkness! After telling this story I would wait for their reaction; of course it was laughter and a little ridicule. They would joke about the dream I had just told them, I was relieved but still wondered what that weird incident I saw was all about. I was wide-awake, not sleep. For years, I wondered about that strange incident. I was glad that I psyched my brothers into thinking that it was all in a dream. However, my mother would just give me a funny kind of stare; she might have ask a few questions that were more peculiar. Did this person say anything? Did you feel his presence before seeing him? In retrospect, I knew she had her suspicions all along about my having a third eye. She had been around those old folks long before I discovered what a third eye was.

My brothers compared my imagination to a boogieman's fairy tail. Me as a young and impressionable younger brother knew that they must be right. I must grow up past this childish nonsense. So I did. So I thought.

But, the boogieman did not grow up or disappear, he did

not outgrow me, he kept on coming and many nights terrorized me. However, as a young brother trying to retain the respect of his older brothers and to avoid their ruthless ridicule, so I kept the boogieman visits a secret.

Yes, there are other life forms here, the boogieman for sure. I can feel the entire scope of surroundings of physical elements such as running water on up to invisible empires way up in the sky all of which lay claim to earth. I have glimpse a most powerful individual overlord who laid claim to this region as well.

The night came as usual; some of those nights, I could be quickly awakened, on full alert for the slightest sound or movement. The darkest part in the room a certain corner of the closet something was there, I could feel it, just as I did many nights before. The silent intruder just stood in the shadows and stared. His stare was very powerful, I could not only feel someone standing in the closet, I could feel the piercing stare of that something looking at me as well. I lie motionless, still as I could, focusing on the person or thing in the closet, waiting and hoping for one of my brothers to get up for a trip to the bathroom. Later, this thing would just cease to be there, and the feeling of night would return to normal. Another strange thing about this boogieman, he did not hide under the bed waiting to grab my ankles as my brothers said he would. This boogieman was always standing and invisible to the naked physical eye. He would always just stare across the room pass my two brothers looking directly at me in the dark.

There would be hundreds of more nights like this dreaded one. Even worse, I would actually have full physical contact with this mysterious night intruder.

Chapter 5

What I will share with you next is true to the best of my senses, but keep in mind that I comprehend a broader spectrum of unseen realities. And for this I also warn you, for what you are about to subsequently learn will endanger you and your love one's, and it will put them and you instantly at risk.

Since my childhood, I have morphed into something else. That you may truly understand the capabilities of my power, I will briefly share with you an incident that involved one of my invasions into the skies above, into the dominion of secondMan. Deep inside the empire, of the infamous and feared, they who have terror struck the universe for thousands of years, who exist as legends in the chronicles of every nation. People of earth who have encountered them at night fear them and for good reason. For others much more powerful than the nations of the earth all combined unleashing all the arsenals at once will mean nothing to the power of the boogieman. He, the secondMan is the most undisputed overlord of physical space in this immediate galaxy of stars.

The event that I now describe was over forty years in the making. Nevertheless, it happened, and to those of you with a functioning thirdEye, just explain to those who remain blind.

Before this incident, I had many contacts with secondMan. At the time, I did not know him as secondMan but what my brothers and I called or referred to him, then as "the boogieman."

There were plenty of strange things happening in my life but like everyone else even myself, I explained them away or ignored them entirely just to try to make my life seem normal. I ignored the truth, and unseen hidden truth, but nonetheless even an unseen invisible thing can be a reality. I masked many of my real experiences as dreams and dismissed events to my over active imagination.

First, let me explain a rather complicated form of travel. There exists something known as descent-level relocation (DLR.) This mind-to-mind method of travel is used to mind energy transport is effective in reaching other points of reality. This energy related method is not limited to physical distance. The mind itself is are a form of reality that exists on descent-level two. Dreams are mental-matter that exists in the mind. During this mode of travel, I have passed certain people in their mind—to them, they see me as a stranger in their dream. They now have details of me without ever meeting me in physical form. Humans in their present state of emotional instability cannot attain this.

In the next incident that I am about to reveal to you, at the time this incursion took place, I did not know the entire scope of secondMan's empires. I initially thought that the boogieman empire controlled everything just above the earth, but after my invasion, I understood many other specie that reside far beyond our known galaxy fear secondMan, even they proceed with caution if entering the boundary as far out as the realm of our milky way.

Before my first cross over battle with secondMan, there was rumored spreading amongst them about a man, a firstMan, with a third eye or as known by them as the eyrefle(those that see the unseen), a man over time has become able to resist their paralysis field, resist the paralysis fields? This feat is in itself impossible. Normally, a man is not able to resist the paralysis fields. This was not the only phenomenon I was capable of, as the boogieman would soon discover in a most unfortunate way.

I had also developed a method that escaped their monitoring capabilities. Through the years of secret, intense, focus and concentration, I became more than an ordinary man. The secondMan would soon discover that not all was predictable in war and so would I.

This incident will begin with the destruction deep inside the hidden fortress of the ancient overlords most sacred location. This place has been a stronghold of secondMan for thousands of years. One whose name is rectinaHost also known as the dreaded and undisputed first lord occupied it. These beings receive their instructions directly from the symbol of the moon only. They, this few elite and ancient overlords ran an entire province extending a light years distance beyond earth. They maintained control of it to the satisfaction of retinaStar.

Finally, my first invasion into the world of the boogieman starts without notice to the naked eye of man. A most startling event occurred, one day my family and I all walked together on a trail at Lensington Park, it was a bright and sunny day, perfect for a stroll my mother was also with us my wife and our two kids Manisha and Cruiser. Suddenly I was hyper-pulled, sped along at a rapid pace through what appeared a dark tunnel. Everything was black until I stopped moving and was standing in a giant doorway. This event took only seconds, my TCR(Terminate Continue Resident) with my family members left in the physical world and as always, I continued my conversations and personality just as though I was really still there in my body with them. No one was aware that my attention had been dispersed elsewhere. Unbeknown to my family, I was still just walking ahead of them enjoying the view. Inexplicably I was able to enter their space, I had tried to achieve this on my own for over forty years, the portal opened. This tall illuminated twenty-foot door was dark sunish transparent yellow in appearance. Finally, I was face to face with the boogieman, my life long adversary. Suddenly within a split second of recognition of each other, first, some, then all of secondMan's military commanders staring at me and me at them; this human crossover to their descent-level was a feat that had not been achieved before. They were caught completely off guard with disbelief. Standing in the restricted top-secret portal opening was not one of their usual comrades, but a man. I immediately felt their thoughts of aggression. Several of the semi-giants leaned over their instrument devices—ever monitoring, ever scanning the minds of man. They had come perhaps for the first time in their lives to be face to face with a man in their own place. More so, a man who had been previously terrorized by them many nights in the past. Some of the hostiles made a lightning fast scramble for their weaponry. Others of the small garrison would try escaping maneuvers, but it was all too late and completely futile. Within that same split second, the room went very black. My defensive weapons of destruction activated. As I slowly walked their military stronghold, deafening thunder filled the compound and flashes of nuclear lightning continuously flowed from my presence. The place shook, and vibrated in deep bass sounding muffled tones. The compound trembled and rocked continuously as echo after echo of muffled arcs of electricity found its victim and annihilating its target. There were no groans of agony. Those who tormented me as a child was now facing doom. If they had restrained themselves and not taken pleasure in terrorizing the innocent all those years, they would have avoided their fate. Some of the destroyed had live for thousands of years and for the first time have saw dismilatinctomcu(death) among them.

Immediately after the lighting stopped the huge black clouds dissipated just as fast as they appeared. Then silence. What I saw afterward was astounding. I found myself looking down, I saw enormous devastation. My right foot frozen in mid step dangled over the edge of a straight down sheared off cliff, one more step and I would have fallen into the pit myself. My esoteric lessons of self-control and adherence to the slightest command I learned from DayStar and the cloud hosts has immediately paid off. Slowly my eyes panned up, where the room and rectinca previously stood was now a great gorge, a huge hole from horizon to horizon in its place. Around the entire edge of the crater was an uncountable number of secondMan—the boogieman. Hundreds of thousands lethargically hanging onto the cliffs edge and some hanging on to others, many lost their lethargic grip and fell into the pit. I looked down as the blinding glowing redness slowly subsided I saw many more had already fallen and lay on top of one another in a great pile of entanglement. I can best describe this from what my interpretation of what we here would think hell looks like.

A commotion interrupted my focus, my attention was drawn to a disturbance of voices emanate above to my right, others were entering, millions of doors in the sky above were opening, I sensed they knew who I was, and one even sensed me as his brother. Brother? I ignored his message and rightfully so, like I said earlier, they know everything about every one here, a one second ploy of distraction is all they need to gain an advantage in the human mind. They started to descend pouring down like rain in a rush to aid their many fallen.

I just witness nothing like I had ever imagined not even from my secret inventions could I achieve something like this. What I just witnessed was no technology of my own. I felt I was really present during the attack, but this was not anything I had conceived prior to this destructive incident.

There was a seamless TSR return back to the park. Again, my family did not suspect anything. Because of the TSR (TransRelocate Stay Resident) permitted me to maintain normal behavior while my mind persona was conducting military missions elsewhere. Also, I practiced a habitual law to keep things secret. No one knew of this war or the others conflicts were about to unfold. Besides, what use could they be? Reflecting on my great power and destruction recently dealt to rectina, I thought myself dukamaduka (invincible in both worlds.)

Over the years I learned the secret to breaking their paralyzing power.

I have since captured the rod of iron from great gatekeeper leadradriama of the outer realm. Nearly fifty years old now, my reputation keep them at bay. I have no fear yet they fear me. I must practice my destruction techniques on thin air for none of them dare come even close to me anymore. I am undisputed except by he who sit upon the secret seat and hide himself in clouds, This ruler himself have not confronted me though I have confronted his image in the form of a giant beige saber-toothed tiger once.

Now you see why you must listen, these people secondMan

are very powerful and now very angry, as I would later find out in the worst way. My undisputed self-given title was premature.

To those of you that have already felt the power of their presence I will tell you this, we have only days to prepare ourselves for their reprisal. I regret my incursion into their abode and the massive destruction that was inflicted. What I did was similar to a man hitting a hornet's nest. You hit the one nest or hornet that stung you, only later to find yourself swarmed by the combatant hornets of the hive. We are about to feel the full power of those that occupy earths hidden six moons. Who are well capable of terrorizing the entire galaxy. You must warn others as soon as you can. I sensed their very angry empire; they are abundant and they extend far out beyond our known galaxy. They will infiltrate earth using descent-level portals. These are the doors I mentioned earlier that I saw opening as they poured down from the skies above. But before their fleets attacks earth in retaliation for my insurgence, they would pay my family a personal visit.

Chapter 6

I have had many conflicts with dukureta legions and they are amazed at my power, even to the throne of satmicata himself. His symbol in the form of a saber tooth tiger larger than two hundred foot high trees once tested me for courage and he knew we feared not one another. I have not been bothered by the boogieman for a long spell after infiltrating their strong hold and destroying many of them. They terrorized me when I was just a kid, but not anymore because I have become dcatolumana (rain of terror) to their empire, now they remain at bay.

I have seen the size of the empire of one known as repsantic's(dark cloud.) with my own eye's, this overlord's domain stretched from horizon north to south, east to west, a dark cloud making it known to me and all that could understand that "he rule here"! I speak of the stars in the sky, not earth's immediate sky.

I have had invisible warriors come to do my family harm, and me some on what seem to be one-way suicide missions; they hurl their rod of iron with force, power and accuracy. My family member suffered.

After my many wars, attacks, and counter attacks I was left alone for a long while. I concluded that they were afraid and the boogiemen had not seen death of their comrades for hundreds even thousands of years and I might even surmise that they had eliminated it completely using various forms of bio-energy mind extraction technology. I took it that they were indeed devastated, and devastated they were, because not long after that I got a visit unlike, I never had before.

Lying in bed one late night, I felt one of them, an unmarked soldier of the mMutota-duku materialized from out of nowhere. By the time my detection field activated he was already to close. I do mean he advanced with such swift speed that was accompanied with a loud noise that penetrated the outer realms of our universe. A noise that if I was in my human state would surely make me deaf. The closest thing I can come to describing it is a screeching sound magnified a thousand times and being quickly charged up getting progressively louder and louder in seconds.

All of a sudden, I could sense his presence, his position, his form, and then "crack"! A loud noise was sent through the house as he planted his feet on the foyer tile located in the hallway. He was poised to hurl his rod of destruction with immense force down the hall to my bedroom… no…to my daughters' bedroom. This all was so unprecedented, never before had the boogieman made a physical entrance into my world with intent to do immediate harm. What was even more disturbing about this episode was that the boogieman knew he would not make it out alive. He knew this was a one-way mission. He was ready to sacrifice himself for something. At the time I did not see the damage his rod of death had done. I would find out the next day that he had indeed found his mark. And oh yes, he was on a suicide mission because after I realized that he was not just here to test my paralysis breaking abilities. I was too late in reacting to his lightning speed action, and the rod was hurled. With great force with great fierceness was it thrown. He threw it with all he had. He meant to deliver maximum damage, as much collateral destruction as possible.

In the past I have capture such rods of power as they were hurled at me on occasion. But this one I could not even see it in flight, nor did I see it hit its intended target. This was a different kind of boogieman. This was a boogieman of vengeance. I was beginning to discover another reason they are so feared throughout the galaxy.

Only seconds after that, someone else, another hidden entity would interfere and inflict a wound of sudden death to the boogieman. I did what I normally do to resist them when they would intrude at night. However, this time I saw a quick flash of dim light that appeared on the wall in the hallway. The introduction of this light during my boogieman visits had never occurred before.

The fatally wounded boogieman survived for only a few minutes. He moved down the hall towards the closet at the north end of the house. He moaned in agony with his mortal wound. I was headed down the hall to finish him off but, I felt a warning from another invisible entity and the warning was so strong it stopped me in my tracks. Despite this warning, I continued to proceed down the hall, but again I was warned to heel! I stood in one spot staring down the hall in the dark, and the moaning noise of a wounded boogieman filled the house and occasional vibrated it. The moan got softer and softer and finally ceased. This event lasted several minutes. After the incident was over, many questions entered my mind. I wondered about the burst or flash of light I saw on the hallway wall. What was this thing or person I felt keeping me from going down the hall? Just when I thought that I understood what was going on more unexplained things were still happening in my life. I also know that I need no new weapons, but I do need to develop some kind of military partneship, I begn to relize that I needed serious help. There are just too many of them, even with a near nuclear lightning bolt, I am no match to the immense boogiemen empire.

They retaliated, for the insurgence I made into their domain. I begin to get nervous again during the night. My enemy had me significantly out numbered, and they had for the first time shown signs of equal determination. They sent a warrior willing to sacrifice and die in battle—not just another cowardly terrorist standing in the closet.

That following morning yes, the tile in the foyer was actually cracked. The floor tile remains broken to this day. He may have come to do even more damage than what he was able to accomplish. Maybe something else intercepted him and cut his mission short. Something was very different about this event with secondMan. He was reacting not like a beastly boogieman but more like a person who sought revenge for losing a loved one or something. He was reacting just like me. When I felt my family threatened. The boogieman was becoming more human like. Could this boogieman be part of a family? I had many new questions.

Chapter 7

You know, the ones who come to you at night, terrorize you, and hold you paralyzed. You tell your spouse, family members, doctor, and they all dismiss it as a dream or poor blood circulation. However, I must ask, does poor circulation have a physical face, the face of a skeleton head?

Unbeknown to me, my ordinary childhood would take a dramatic turn. This would start with a strange visitor that came only during the night. I had to abruptly leave my childhood because I was faced with an uncommon enemy. No police could help, I could not go to the government, nor any of its first-line of defense agencies. I thought of going straight to the US military several times for help, or at least alert them to what I knew, but two things stopped me. One, an inner voice warned me to say nothing, and two, civilization in any military capacity had no chance against the likes of the boogieman. As I have said many times before, the boogieman is more than a spook in the dark; he is more powerful then you will ever know.

Yes, since my childhood my mind has traveled far to the ends of realmmacpia(end of physical space), but I have returned with undivided attention, I have a warning to evil…be warned! In addition, a message to my brothers, the boogieman is real!

My childhood ceased when I was about five years old. Since that time I have been at the business of survival and tactical maneuvering against a most uncommon enemy of mankind.

Again, many nights would come and go without incident. I began to think perhaps I had outgrown my childhood imagination. Yeah, that is it; the boogieman was just a figure of my young imagination. Now at eighteen, I'm practically a full adult. Besides, I now lifted weights and was physically built. I practiced karate, boxing and jujitsu; the boogieman had gone for a long time. However, on one particular summer night, an unprecedented thing happened; my imagination would merge with my reality.

The hour was around midnight, as I returned from the toilet passing my mother's room and the stairway then to my bedroom, as I had I done countless of times before without incident. I remember well the sounds I heard that night, the noise of my older brother talking in the basement with his best friend named Vincer who was playing the bongos. I stopped long enough to pick up the rhythm that pounded the drums. Bongo playing was another one of my favorite pastimes. I even bought my conga drum and played it nearly every night sitting on the back porch. As I was saying, I went on back to my room, climbed into bed to get more sleep. Then suddenly from nowhere he came. He was back! This time not confined to the darkest areas of the closet or corners in my room. This visit was up close and in my face! No sooner than I hit the mattress laying down on my right side, a pressure, from some full-grown man with a strong grip grabbed my left wrist. He was right at my bedside kneeling behind me. I was paralyzed even before the grip. A grip so strong I could not jerk away. He had returned! I had forgotten about him. He was more powerful then before and I suddenly realized that I had not outgrown him. Even without seeing who this intruder was I could once again feel the old piercing stare I felt as a kid years before. It was the boogieman!!! Yes, my childhood imagination came back and had gotten worse. This night I will again experience my old childhood terror, panic, heart pounding, and rapid breathing. I tried, but I could not call to by brother for help. If only I could call out…but I couldn't I could not move, not even a finger! This time it was very different because my imaginary boogieman came in physical contact with me. After a while still gripping firmly on my wrist, the intruder allowed me to move, I still was not permitted to speak or even blink, but I was permitted to slowly rotate and turn my head, slowly, toward my captor's direction. I was even further terrorized when I started to make out the shape of someone's head coming into view. His eyes were more like eye sockets. Continually turning, I then found myself staring face to face, into what looked like a man with a stocking over his face. Man shaped head with dark sunken eye sockets, no eyeballs like ours. He kneeled next to my bed, holding me motionless with his paralytic power while keeping a firm grip on my left wrist. He stared close up in my face. Only this was not my imagination. I would later discover that this is the same boogieman that had come and terrorize me so many nights when I was a kid.

The medical professionals mis-diagnosed this experience as poor blood circulation. The medical experts are wrong!

My world was shattered. I could not discuss this with my teachers, my mother, my brothers, or anyone. I knew that I was dealing with some distorted bully, a despicable kind of life form other than human, an evil that surpass the evil of human malevolence by comparison. Even with one of my older brothers nearby and I being fully awake, did not prevent this physical invasion. No, the boogieman had now crossed the physical threshold, never had he done this. We now had physical contact with one another. I was afraid, and he was letting me know to be afraid. Today, I do not need the medical profession mis-diagnosis. I have re diagnosed and remedied the issue myself. I established the fact that life is not an imagination, you may have an imaginary thing like Santa Clause or the Easter Bunny, but no matter what you call it the boogieman, demon, or the devil, I assured myself from that point on that my realities were real. The definition of reality is not what you choose to exist but what exist despite your denial of existence.

I was faced with a real unearthly problem, none of my inventions helped against such a foe. None of the things I tried to create over the years helped. Nothing could stop them, believe me when I tell you as I have mentioned before, I did not consider the US or Russian military as a threat, and remember I was just a kid about fifteen or sixteen years old. By that time, I had developed many secret devices. However, against this foe, nothing that I created would help. Because my weapons were of a physical nature, I needed a new technology; something that could liberate me from their paralyzing force would be a start. I also recall the power of his vise like grip; he was very physically strong far beyond human motor mechanics. Contact with him, felt more like a giant reptile or hard ant like crustacean material. No human is capable of hand-to-hand combat with these creatures of the night. In addition, this person did not maintain a consistent physical form. Because just as fast as he physically entered my room, he could just as quickly vanish. During most of the boogieman's intrusions, I learned to covertly detect and monitor his activities. I even began to marvel at his technology to paralyze the human mobility system. He could walk through walls, I began to wonder… he seemed intent to do great harm, but for some other reason he would not or was it that he could not. The next day I told no one what happened that night.

That same morning my mother told us about a stranger in her room, she tried all she could to fight him but could not succeed.

Chapter 8

But as far back as I can recall other strange things occurred. As always I would passed them off as my overactive imagination. Just as my friends, family members and teachers had made me believe. I was dreadfully wrong. The things that I am telling you happened. Next are the symbols, which I learned about later, the secondMan, mMutota and tenanokatonon.

One time back in our old original residence around 1962, we lived in the high-rise apartments or what people called the projects. Our apartment was on the twelfth floor, the unit and address number was 1281 Seldom Street.

I did not know nor dare I say this was not my regular boogieman. But what happened then would later shed light on events and beings on this entire story.

One night being jolted from sleep my attention was drawn to a pile of clothes to my left in a chair that sat by our bedroom door. I had a strange feeling about the cloths and therefore continued staring at them. Then the pile of clothes slowly morphed into a full-grown male lion. He just sat there licking his paws he stared straight forward as though he could not see me. After I collected myself from under the covers, I peeked out to find that the lion was gone and only the pile of clothes remained. I woke up everyone in the house that night to tell them what I was.

My mother again had that strange look on her face as not to discourage me, but at the same time trying to camouflage thae fact she may have known something. As time went on

I began to re-analyze those looks, did she really know something that I did not know? Was she hiding something herself? Because it seems that her questions were always, just enough not feed into my hysteria but enough to decide a certain amount of truth you think you perceived. Maybe even to confirm some of her own unexplained encounters she was experiencing.

Thinking back, I never felt fear of the lion. I never felt evil intent nor hate from his presence. I only saw him once. Later, I would know what this symbol meant—The Great Lion. A Great protector, but for what reason would such a all-powerful thing be needed? Moreover, more interestingly, why was his symbol projected here in a non-important ghetto? How truly serious was the threat we faced? How powerful was our enemy who lingered and followed us from the distant shadows? I would later come to know the boogieman's might and the power of the invisible ever-watchful lion.

Chapter 9

As a teenager, I had mentally conjured up a lot of top-secret invention to dangerous to share with anyone. I had sense enough not to write any of this far-out stuff down, ever! Even, now, I will never tell of many of the devices I created because they can do such great harm.

At any rate, it seems my boogieman was way more powerful than before and he was ready to deliver as much damage to me as possible. There was a war being contemplated and waged between an uncommon enemy and me. I would be unimpressed at the daily news reports about the USSR and US. I had my hand full with a foe I was sure could easily destroy them all if it were not for the loathsome benefit he harvested from man at night. Anyway, the threat of war between our two super powers would have to take a back seat. I had more serious things to consider now. I would create devices that far surpassed than what has been developed here for armed conflict. I created these weapons to prevent this clear and physical threat from the boogieman, after all this boogieman asked for conflict when he terrorized my mother. Terrorizing me is one thing but mess with someone's mother? Where we grew up everyone even the local bully had intellect enough not to mess with or talk about someone's mother. Playtime was over. I was going to devise a way to kill the boogieman. This would take me on a path that led to some of the most awesome sciences imagined. I deconstructed what I had seen him do and then used all my resources to re-create his power and technology.

I came close to duplicating the boogieman's paralyzing field. From this point, I turned my undivided attention to the invisible evil that stalked me and now obviously my mother. This person or thing had what my elementary school music teacher named Mr. West called "my undivided attention".

I would spend many years trying to emulate his technology with no success. No matter how hard I tried, I could not completely duplicate the paralysis fields or the invisible state that he maintained. No matter, when he would come, I would try to fight and resist him; I would face him eye to eye eventually with not a molecule of fear in my heart. I wanted to get to him but could not. This bastard's technology was too different, to great. I still needed something else. However, there was nothing else, at least not here on earth anyway.

To defeat my foe I needed something not of this world, something not of a physical nature. My devices worked only on physical things like people, animals etc. not on him the boogieman. My magnetic light-bending device rendered me invisible here; my brothers did not even know I was in the room standing in the closet with this thing on. The miniature motors silenced by vacuum-sealed compartments (A thing I nearly slipped and told Mr. Hains about in my Physics class once) I had torn the small landing apart in the closet and concealed this device inside. No one knew it was there. Our shoes sat on top of it all the time. I had bio welded it so it could not be opened without tearing the wood itself apart. But, this device was no match for my enemies. His was somehow mobile, self-contained, portable or maybe even biophysimental. It apparently had or at least showed no moving parts. He was not restricted to a certain spot. In addition, his seemed to have the option to work on a specific mind-light frequency so restricting only certain persons to see him even though others might be in the same vicinity. The room, the environment did not change, in every instance it remained the same hence leading me to conclude that this was in fact a real experience versus some imaginary creation. The boogieman could enter my mind and my physical matter. My formidable adversary's technology permitted him to transverse two realities.

And though I lived everyday like a normal person, on the inside, inside my mind, I was using my terrorist's frequent contacts with him to study him, to get to know more about him, his technologies and military implications.", I often wondered why the boogieman seemed interested in only certain people. What seemed to be a desperate and necessary intrusions of terror to get me or stop me from doing or achieving something though not obvious to me but; very obvious to him. Each encounter with the boogieman would yield more and more information about him and his technology. He would attack only the mind and was not interested in the physical body itself. It was as though to him the mind or something in the mind was more important then the body or maybe even the mind itself. I was reminded of a saying in boxing, yes; I spent my share of time boxing as a child. The saying goes "kill the head and the body will die" My nemesis seemed to have a similar motto "kill the mind or destroy something in the mind, and the truth dies".

In years of observing the boogieman, there is one inescapable conclusion, earth, our planet, us falls under the realm of a vast and powerful invisible evil empire.

I have given you much detail about the unseen conflict between two very different beings, one is physical and the other the boogieman consisting of multi-matter. At the time, it seemed I would remain under their hidden power, threaten by them at will. But the universe is a vast place and I came to realized that it was full of beings separated by great distance. Distances of epic scale, because there exist what I can best describe as layers or levels. One life form could exist and not be aware of another in the same period but at different levels. The being on the upper level can see the one on the lower but not vise versa. One has then a distinct advantage over the other. If ever I needed an ally of greater power something from another place, not of this world, I need that something now if I am ever going to stand a chance against my boogieman foe. You don't understand how fully powerful the boogieman is until I tell you he once withstood, though for only a short period the force of a power I can best define as omnipotent, and there are many such beings, and that he did. This alone is a testament to his tremendous, unseen power. I no longer underestimate him.

I know I am covering a lot of territory but precedence is necessary. For I only have just a short time to warn you. I will continue in such manner of telling the story for it is just a matter of the time.

Chapter 10

There was something I found puzzling about the boogieman's behavior over the years. My answer would come only as time unfolded. The opening of the eye is a long and arduous process sometimes. However, later I began to see there were different conduct and motives from the uninvited invisible strangers that entered into my home.

Over the years there were countless scuffles not battles because there was nothing I could physically do to the boogieman. There would be long spans of time between his visits or attempted attacks. I had married and had a beautiful little daughter. My wife and I stayed with my mother for several months before deciding to move into our own place. We looked and searched around, even trying some of those apartment rental companies. We would drive around for days on end looking in the north of the city and the west. The Apartment service list had mostly cruddy choices in our opinion. We eventually located a nice recently built apartment complex located not far from my mother. My wife and I moved in, decorated the place. Her mother and sisters helped with the choice of furniture. There was the kitchen furniture, which her mother bought for us. What a blessing. My wife and I chose the living room furniture. The bedroom furniture was from other members of the family. I decorated the walls with smoked mirrors and cork. The kitchen floors covered with an outdoors carpeting tile. Life was very normal. I had a good job, a wife and a beautiful child…and then a surprise visitor from an old friend. Once again, over time I had begun to forget. Only this time, I was not the intended victim. After a normal day of work, we both picked up the baby from the baby sitter. We then ate dinner, watched a little TV to keep updated on current events, and then went to bed. My wife nicknamed "sweetie" would liked to talk a lot just before bedtime. She would talk about improving the apartment, things that she would like doing on the weekend like shop. She would talk energetically then suddenly she would get sleepy. It was my job then to always to have to get up out my comfortable bed and turn out the light. We would snuggle briefly and both would eventually fall a sleep.

Honey! Ike! Ike! Ike! There is a man in the house! My heart pounded, the blood rushed to my head. The morning light hit my eyes; I squinted until my eyes adjusted the bright sunny light. An intruder, my mind raced to our daughter who was only three month old at the time in the other room right next to ours. First creeping out the bed I crawled, checking our closet, then in the bathroom, then sprinted into her room, bring her to our room placing her in bed with my wife, my wife who clearly was somewhat shaken but more calmed after seeing that our daughter was all right. I asked her quietly, what did you see? She explained, "I woke up and a man was standing in the doorway. From that I wasted no more time for any further details, there was possible an intruder in the house and I had to protect my family. I grabbed an item for a weapon and getting into the mode of self-defense, which I learned through all the years of practicing martial arts. I would get this intruder. This was a very small apartment with only two small rooms, one bathroom, kitchen, a kitchenette and the living room. There was only one entry, the front door in the living room. My intruder would be trapped with no quick way to escape. After getting my daughter, I stared down the hall to the front door. I inched back to my daughter's small room, with a quick look around. I proceeded to the bathroom, checking behind the door looking through the crack at the hinges knowing that nobody was there or could be hiding there still, not leaving anything to chance; I lightly pushed the door back anyway. I check the kitchen, the living room, behind the sofa bed, every closet and the pantry. The intruder had somehow escaped. The immediate danger was gone. Now standing upright, I walked back to the room "did you see anyone"? My wife asked. No, no one, nothing" I replied. I stayed in the bed and rubbed her back and shoulders. To further console her the best I could. This man, what did he look like I asked, what did you see? She said, he was somewhat short; he had on a dark looking uniform or something. A uniform I asked. Yes. I remember asking her about the bedroom door, like do she recall it being already open or did the intruder push it open, the intruder pushed it open after first poking his head in. I also recall getting up going to the front door. The front door has a chain lock on it. The beauty about this lock is that it did not lock from the outside. Someone on the inside of the apartment could secure the latch. My intruder managed to come in my home, and leave, without needing to lock or unlock the doors. I returned to the room to ask my wife some more questions. Are you sure you saw someone? Yes! She nervously replied. I explained to her that the door was still latched. Tell me again what you saw, from the beginning. Well, I was sitting here in the bed just thinking, "you were all ready woke I interrupted?" Yes! She replied. This man poked his head in the door, I was confused because I had just looked at you sleeping and knew you were in the bed lying next to me. The man then walked over to the bed, stood right next to your bedside and looked down as though he never even knew I was in the room. That is when I yelled to wake you up. "Then what happened I asked?" He just walked right out the window she replied. I know this sounds crazy she rushed to say. Quickly, I attempted to calm her down to assure her that she was not crazy. It is time to share the secret life that I have kept hidden. It was perhaps time I told her about a childhood imaginary thing that I could somehow I never out grew. I would tell her of the infamous boogieman. Not going into all the gory scary details, but enough to let her think that I was familiar with her experience and that there was nothing to really worry about.

Chapter 11

Inwardly I was furious. This boogieman had now invaded my new family. There was hostility and angry in my blood, the determination to destroy had returned. Nevertheless, there was something bothering me about her boogieman. There was something different about her boogieman. One, she never expressed any feelings of hate or evil emanating from this boogieman, Two, this happened while she was wide-awake, and three most interesting, she recalled that this man had a insignia of some kind on the chest plate of his uniform. The other differences I had noticed, she did not speak of his face, as I have described my boogieman having dark sunken eye sockets. Her descriptions she without hesitancy spoke of a "man" and even more astonishing the boogieman did not immobilize her with the paralyze field. She was able or permitted to move, scream or what ever she wanted to do. Strange, very strange I thought as the day passed.

Firstly, this is a new being that can walk through walls and render him invisible. Secondly and most profound, this new boogieman appears in the daytime? The daytime...all of my boogiemen intrusions occurred at night!

This called for a new revolutionary hypothesis. There were perhaps two kinds of boogiemen, one evil and one not so evil? Maybe, this boogieman was the lesser evils, but nonetheless evil for sure! Because all boogiemen are evil…right? Now it appeared to be more than one type of boogiemen. Different or not, my determination increased to discover a way to finally abolish this person, this thing. He terrorized me in the worse way. He visited my new family putting everything at risk. I needed a strategy, some kind of unearthly force, but up till now there was none. This incident made me ponder that question: are there possibly two types of boogiemen? I recalled an incident my mother had revealed to me several days earlier. She told me about a pair of strange intruders that had mysteriously entered her bedroom. One was very evil with evil intent; the second intruder was more powerful than the first. I listened with great interest as she elaborated on the details.

Chapter 12

Nearly every day after work I would stop by to visit my mother. One day she told me about one of her encounters that forced me to reconsider the possibility of the unprecedented multiple boogiemen theory.

We were both standing in the living room downstairs talking when we heard this very heavy person placed both feet on the floor, the floor actually squeaked under the extreme weight of this person. I looked at my mother and quickly asked her who was upstairs, no one she immediately replied. I ran up the stairs, this was a two story home, to look into her bedroom; I searched the closets and for the first time noticed that there was an attic door in the closet ceiling. Again, being thorough and a good investigator, I got a chair and stood on it to get a closer look at the door only to determine that the paint that sealed the door shut had never been broken. The person the obviously weighed several hundred of pounds did not escape into the attic. I found nothing. No one was hiding upstairs.

After I came back down stairs, she proceeded to tell me about a dream she had that night. She said while laying in bed something, or some being came to mess with her. She explained how she became very angry; she could not fight this thing, needing help she prayed. Abruptly she said, someone flew into the window and this something that was tormenting her flew out the room. The man who flew into her window sat down in the chair next to her bed. After that, she felt calm and she fell asleep. I recognized this experience for I knew that this being was in fact the infamous boogieman.

I recognized this diversion trick well, you know, concealing a real experience into a fictitious dream. I myself often employ the term of having "a dream" when in fact describing experiences that I considered real.

I have often wondered about the second boogieman or could I refer to this apparent new boogieman as type-2, he was not acting like the traditional boogieman at all.

With what my wife and mother have told me I started to get a better profile of the inhabitants of the unseen world.

Remember the lion in the chair I spoke of earlier? The one in my bedroom transformed from a pile of clothes. Strange as all this sounded to a normal person, even to a normal person it would later start to make sense. To unfold a hidden world and hidden unseen truth was a long tedious process. Who were these new type-2 boogiemen? All intruders generate fear, but not as threatening as the evil boogieman. I did not immediately make the connection regarding the boogieman types because being that these incidents slowly unfolded over a period of fifty years.

I immediately saw the similarity between the two boogiemen that my wife had described and what my mother had told me. My mother's boogieman like that of my wife's could go right through walls, remain invisible if preferred, did not scare her with an evil persona like the first boogieman, nor did her boogieman paralyze her. It was becoming clear that there were different kinds of beings, one the boogieman and the other, should I be saying the boogieman. The question now is what type of being is this second boogieman? The two boogiemen did not act the same and they did not share the same goals with their visitations. The bad boogieman appeared only in the dead of night and in the darkest corner of a room, he entered. The difference seemed so strikingly opposite that a new name had to be established. A radical conclusion was interjected because of my future encounters with this second being, which I called the guardian. I not only saw this being but I saw many all at one time in the worse way. Things were starting to happen indeed and at an accelerated pace.

One may wonder how I made the connection between the lion in a chair to guardian in a chair. It was not until later that I understood that some specie communicate in symbols. They used familiar things to communicate, like the images they read from your mind, and then feeding the likeness back to your mind as a representation of their purpose or being.

Chapter 13

As time passed and I was able to glimpse more of the unseen than before. I began to mentally detect the scope of an empire that resided overhead in the sky. A vast empire with traveling machines traversing the skies overhead in the blink of an eye. When these momentary events occurred, I pretended as though I did not see anything at all. Sometimes the ability to sense the empire would just happen without my control or anticipation.

There are rings that extend from earths moon to reach beyond our solar system. These artificially created rings were used primarily for mind scanning and to maintain a safe parameter from other beings with hostile intent to their empire. Minds that register a certain mental pattern were not permitted to enter within the realm. In addition, the earth has many moons. The moon we all can see with the naked eye our human eye. When permitted to perceive with my third eye, I witnessed many moons of various sizes orbiting the earth.

I began to wonder, what is it that the boogieman is doing during his stealth visits to our bedsides? How long has he been here, visiting earth? At first, he seemed more like an alien than human. But as I had more contact I began to surmise that the boogieman is more humanlike in some conduct than appearance would have led me to believe. The intense remark I felt or heard one exclaimed "Brother!" as he entered the destructive aftermath I inflicted years before still reverberates in the back of my mind. "Brother?" What was the true meaning of this statement? Years passed before I would get my first life shattering eye-opening clue.

Chapter 14

I am the unoducata—rainier of terror. But by now we all know in my early years this was not always been the case. I use to be a simple ordinary person, but over time, I have morphed into something else. My life began as a young boy growing up in a major city, more specifically in a city named Detroit, Michigan.

So that you will better understand I am one of us with the same sentiments as you, I had the same experiences as many of you. Let me briefly tell of my childhood or what seemed at the time an ordinary childhood. In actuality, this period of my life was the groundwork being prepared for a different kind of adulthood or should I say function. All I thought of was going outside and playing after school like other children. During this early period of my life, I knew nothing of the mMutota, the son's of Tenakatonon, anioDomino or function calls.

In the summer during my elementary school years, like any other kid, I could not wait for summer break. I could not wait to get up early in the mornings to go out and catch insects. My friends and I would meet on the 12th floor in the stairwell of our apartment building. There would be the long review of everyone's insect collecting hardware, jars with holes punched into the lids so all the newly captured insects could breath, nets, white curtain material sewed on to a coat hanger bent into a circle and attached to the end of a broom handle. We would strategize and outline our parameter as to where we would catch the best insects. This excursion began with a race down twelve flights of steps, while holding onto the banister when some of us would jump four, eight, even fifteen stairs at a time. Sometime an entire flight of stairs was achieved with one hand sliding the stair rail. Following each completed flight was a loud thump as our shoes and boots hit the bottom of the landing. The smaller kids taking only one and two stairs at a time made rapid but none-the-less the same loud noises in attempt to keep pace with there older brothers and friends. At the end of our stair running campaign, busting carelessly through one heavy steel door, once out of the dimly lit stairwell, a quick rush through the vest-view we were all outside standing in front of the apartment building. The cacophony of excited chatter was mixed with the occasional car horn and siren in the distance.

As we walked to our destination, we exchanged potato chips, cakes and pop back and forth between some of the hungry members of our group. Snacks were devoured in great haste, because there were no grown ups around to caution us about how fast or how much to eat, or in what order to eat the cake before the sandwich or vise versa. The choice and pleasure was all ours. Food gave way as we approached a wide street called Stimpson, so-called on the west side and Myrtle on the eastside. This was not the widest biggest street in our area but certainly one that required the warnings from parents and our undivided attention as younger members were watched carefully and told exactly when to cross. First, some older kids sprinted across without regard or fear for the cars, and then when all was absolutely all clear, autos caught by a red light, everyone sprinted across both lanes toward the empty lots across the street.

Immediately after crossing this landmark street and the sidewalk, climbing the chain-linked fence, then jumping to the ground, we were in the thicket of the overgrown grass and tall weeds. We would stand there surveying each his plot or territory, deciding which direction would yield the best and biggest insects. Some weeds in various patches were taller then us, but not enough to block or obscure our view, most of the huge field consisted of shorter vegetation of wild growth about knee-high. The smell of different odors of grass, weeds, and foliage was always a most welcomed scent. The sounds of the many different insects chirping noises and buzzing sounds, along with the many various flying insects (some bristly rushing right by one's very ear) was enough to get me over excited. I could not wait to discover what would be revealed by kicking through the tall grasses. There was no organized method to catching or disturbing the inhabitants of the insect world. Everyone generally went his own way, some would trek alone and those who were best friends stayed together. I remember there were some days I would track down big giant grasshoppers, some so energetic they could wear me down in trying to keep track of their escape maneuvers. They would hop and fly veering right then left several times and stay in flight for long distances. Upon landing, the big brownish grasshopper would fold his yellow and black wings, land then quickly turn to watch us approach his new location. This routine would continue for several minutes with some of the king sized insects. Then eventually, his flights became shorter and shorter, slower and slower, we would get closer and closer. Slowing down and being very cautious, we approached and with a quick swing of the net, "bingo", we got him! What a great feeling, to add such a big trophy to your collection. We were very excited because this was the biggest catch of the group. The younger kids would yell out with exuberating over the size of the catch. Some would catch all the bees they could; others would wait to find the all green grasshopper… the katydid. The katydid was truly a prize for several reasons, one, it was different rather than being brown it was bright green, two some of them were quit large, and most of all at night, it created a loud buzzing sound by rapidly shaking his wings. This would keep everyone staring at this prized jar for hours on end until the streetlights came on which then some of the kids would break into a sprint for home, even neighborhood bullies. The streetlight coming on was a universal signal for most of us that it was time to come in before nightfall. If your mother had to call you beyond this point, this could mean trouble. Those who followed the unwritten law to the letter were also the brunt of many street light jokes. The turning on of the streetlights always signaled the end of another exciting summer day, which continued throughout the whole summer, long days and short nights. The summer would always end too quickly.

From chasing and catching insects to inventing modified army toys, one of my other more notable childhood adventures occurred at school. Thinking back, it was a clear indicator of my hidden inventiveness capabilities. At the beginning of a new elementary school year and very early in the morning, my mother would wake us to get us up bright and early. There would be the smell of breakfast hitting my nostrils, sometimes it would be bacon and eggs other times it would be pancakes and French fries—my favorite. Our clothes would be ironed to razor sharp, our shoes freshly polished, but before we could rush to put on our clothes we would have to wash—what a waste of time. First, my sister, then down the line of brothers, me being last. I would then rush to woof down my good breakfast, grab my bags, and run out the door. When going to school, most of the times I would use the elevator and it would be loaded with other kids. My brothers and I lived our separate lives for sure when it came to school. I would never see them going to, during, or returning from school. For a very short period, we all attended the same elementary school because there was only two years ages difference between the three of us.

School was also normal, I had science, art, music, math classes, and of course gym period, which was my favorite period. I loved to climb the rope and touch the ceiling, then slide back down. I was amazed at the guest firefighters that visited our school that could climb the rope military style using only their hands, climbing with their hands overlapping one over the other with their legs spread out not touching the rope as they climbed. After gym class came lunch, oh boy, what I liked most about this time was the little small glass bottles of milk. They had a cardboard lid that you peeled off, inserted your straw, and then I would drink the milk to my hearts content. This milk tasted better than the store-bought milk we had at home.

Elementary my dear boy… Physics 101:
On the exterior, I was always portraying to be just an average student. However, I do recall some teachers being amazed at my level of comprehending science and its possible impact it can have on society. I recall a more technical incident that occurred during the sixth grade with Ms. Harrison the elementary school science teacher. For a long time, I had taken lots of copper wiring from various electronic devices, radios, TV's, and stereos anywhere I could find wound copper wiring. One day, my older brother's friend name Ellis Harnes notices a box full of copper and went into an excited fit explaining to his mother all the many different kinds of copper I had accumulated. I did not know why I was attracted to copper or other electronic devices. My intent was to make a electronic launching device that would send a marble flying through the air. All the neighborhood kids were using marbles for

their slingshots exertion. Some of them made custom slingshots consisting of 2 X 4 lumbers resembling more of a crossbow. I bought some of the supplies at the Five and Dime store—one of my favorite places to shop. The sound of walking on the old wooden floors and giant blowing fans on hot summer days is most memorable. Most of the time I would go there in many cases just day-dream and look at all the merchandise hanging on the walls, BB guns, air rifles, bow and arrows, archer sets, and spin wheels.

Without ever picking up a book or studying science, I was acutely, aware of how the electronic world worked. My experimenting with magnets, which was another one of my pass time, I already knew that opposites attract and like ends- poles repelled. I knew that my coiled wire was the same as my solid metal magnets because of the way solid metal was identically attracted to the coils when connected to a battery. Although permanent magnets were a great way to pass the time, they however, were much too weak for what I wanted. I needed something much more powerful, stronger, and bigger. I had already observed that when a battery is first connected or disconnected to my coils of wire a magnetic field also was generated. I knew this because during each connect and disconnect our TV would flicker with static. In addition to learning this phenomenon this experiment provided me a lot of fun many of evenings while my family or friends were watching TV. They would spend time adjusting the antenna, various knobs, and of course mumbling under their breath, others even cursing in near silence about this blankie-d-blank TV. All the while it was me hidden in another room purposely causing havoc on the TV located in the living room. This went on for days and months. No one ever knew it was me. Even at that time, I knew the value of a secret. More importantly, I think due to self-preservation I dared not tell now for fear of a “blankie-d-blank” butt kicking from one of my annoyed brothers. They were good for giving you a knuckle-pressing and rolling a knuckle hard against the top of one’s head).

The next thing I needed was a metal marble; hence, my first encounter to what would become one of my most admired things as a kid. I was introduced to what kids in that time called a “steely” Yes; this was solid metal shinny chrome marble. It was the super marble. It was use in marble games only on unsuspecting neophytes. With one flick of the thumb, it could croak an entire patch of marbles. Used skillfully hitting dead center on the edge, it would send all them multicolored marbles flying outside the ring in the sand. The marbles came in many wonderful colors, some were clear, while others called cat-eyes were all clear with a thin slither of colored twisted plastic in its center. Some marbles were solid white with swirls of various patterns on their surface. Whites, reds, yellows, and blues of every kind would be flying in all directions when hit with the force of the “steely”. It would leave the onlookers wide-eyed, jaw dropped and shocked at the power of such an invincible weapon. It was heavy and bigger than traditional marbles. It would require the skill of accurately holding it with the forefinger and nestle snuggly behind the thumb. Nevertheless, once unleashed, all competitors would scramble to grab what marble they could and run, others would quit the game. The kid with the secret super steely, would gather all his new bounty, fill his pockets, bulging with other conquests, and just move on in search of another group of unsuspecting marble players. Ah… do I need one of those!

Thanks to the game of marbles, I now had the super munitions for my new electronic launcher science project.

The “steely” was perfect. It was perfectly round, heavy, and most important, it was made of metal. With some brainstorming, I could finagle this object to react with the magnetic fields… ha ha ha aaaa, I liked being like the mad scientist. Making this ball bearing properly interact with the triggering mechanism was a small challenge. I learned to follow what is known as my first thought (images will flood my mind), If I miss this opportunity I would be left with normal trial and error methods that could take months even years before reaching a solution. Therefore, after visualizing what I needed, I assembled the devices to match the same polarity with the end facing the bearing. When the coil is energized, both the metal and the coils magnetic pole would be the same polarity. Now all I had to do was work out the construction details over the next several days. I completed the project late in the night. After all had fallen asleep, I had quietly removed my weapon from behind some boxes hidden under my bed. There I sat in the middle of the night using only the moon light to proudly observe my new secret weapon “er humm,” I mean toy. Slingshot of all slingshots! Tomorrow, I would introduce to the slingshot game the kind of excitement that the steely had brought to the marble competitions. There would be no other slingshot that could compete with this one. It will surely get me praise from my science teacher Ms. Harrison.

I plan to secretly test it in the house, which if I were caught would surely render me an butt whipping. I waited until everyone is gone, aiming it at a pile of clothes, applying just a little electricity using a smaller coil at first. Then watched as the steely flew from the barrel into the pile of garments, and eventually being stopped by the mattress. My projectile flew out with such force I began to get a little worried. But nothing was going to stop what I was planning for tomorrow. To make a true spectacle, I had rigged a super coil, using a large coil of wire gotten from an old welder. I was planning to replace my low voltage battery with a direct connection to a portable homemade two hundred watt power supply. All of a sudden, my conscience kicks in; there was something dangerous about this toy. I postponed my launch date long enough to add some tape then wrap the steely with many green and brown rubber bands and re-enforce with more tape. When I was done, the thing was big as a golf ball. My thinking was that it would not do serious harm if it hit a person. This also required track modifications. But, because I had the tracks separated by adjustable bolts I could narrow and widen the track to accommodate the different projectile sizes as necessary. I recall sneaking it outside one early morning before all the other kids were came out to play. I had hidden my contraction in an old green Hudson's shopping bag and grocery cart. I thought I had better make a test run before the big unveiling in front of all my friends and competitors alike. So, I set it up outside, carefully aimed it up toward the sky toward another apartment building safely far across two huge fields separating the buildings. A quick re-check of all the components, the bearing, the tracks and a final electrical check. The only thing I had to do was flip the switch and zoom. ZOOM it did! There was the usual recoil but in this case, I knew to brace the launcher up against the wall to prevent exaggerated recoil action. Instead of the thing jumping back, which it could not flip backward, thank God it had already released its projectile. Within a split second, I realized I might have thanked God too early. It released it all right! That rubber coated bearing flew lighting speed across both fields in a straight line up up, up, and crashed into a thirteenth floor window. My eye's bucked like golf balls as in minutes later a young boy came to the window sticking his head out with the curtain now waving out the broken window pane, then his mother came to the window looking all around until she spotted me far across the other side of the complexes. I knew she was thinking that I could not have possibly hurled an object that far, no one could. But I was not thinking straight and was not going take any chances. I quickly grabbed my launcher and recklessly stuffed it into the grocery cart spreading the old worn faded blankets on top to conceal it. First walking then after turning the corner, I ran, until I was back upstairs in my own apartment. I was so afraid; I started to dismantle the device. Occasionally I would look out my window across the field at the other building to see the damage I had done. This device was powerful, no one consider this a toy, it was as my later mind concluded, it was a weapon. This was not like the army games and toy the other kids were all running around playing with. With he device dismantled, I put it back into the box with the other copper. I converted the racks into standard 2X4 slingshots like those that the other kids had. As far as I was concerned, I had avoided a major butt whopping what we called "whipping" from my mother. She was the perfect mother all those years, but even as I got older, stronger, and taller, I still never disrespected her and even feared her in the right way until the point me and my brothers would never even let her hear us mumble a cursing word, not so much as a close similarity like "darn" or "dang." I wasn't about to even find out what kind of "whipping" would be dished out for shooting off a new homemade never seen weapon (I mean science project) across the sky into a neighbors bedroom would get me. As I got older, I realized that the projectile traveled a good several hundred feet upward in a somewhat of an acute angle before crashing into the other building. Also, I recall the amazing speed at which this thing had traveled, nearly as fast as I could plug and then unplug I am talking a split second, before I could look up to see where it was going it had already found and hit its target with enough force after reaching it to knock out the window. Even more amazing, there was hardly any noise when fired, no puff of smoke. This was indeed some kind of weapon with great potential. Yeah, just let the Russians try invading if I am around. As kids, we also liked to play army "let's play army" then all of my friends would go and bring back all of their best army men and war equipment. Even though I knew, I had top-secret weapons I never tired or pre-maturely out grew this kind of fun of playing "army" with my friends.

My impulse to created and build destructive things did not stop there, later on as I grew older I would make other devices, test them, dismantle them and keep them secret. Putting it this way, with all the secret weaponry I was developing I had no fear of anything in this world. Oh yes, except for our mother who stood about five feet plus and weighed slightly over hundred plus pounds.

As for my science project, forget taking the launching device to school because this thing may be able to somehow link me to the incident of the busted window.

So early that morning, I reached down in my trusty box of metals and remove a large hunk of silvery looking metal. This was a piece of alloy taken from an old broken iron my mother had planned to throw away. I mesmerized friends and science colleagues alike with what I called a "piece of solid mercury". I pulled it out in each class to show this amazing piece of mercury I had found and created in my home. One of my friends at the time was a fellow student named Wayne. The teacher questioned about the little disturbance in the back of the classroom, "Ike has a hard piece of Mercury" Wayne relied excitedly. How interesting she responded. My prank was going well I thought. Until I got to science class, Ms. Harrison did not buy it for a minute. This at first, however briefly with a puzzled look on her face and after examining my "piece of hard mercury" then asking me several questions, she explained scientifically, that to become a solid mercury had to be many degrees below zero temperature and in this frozen state could not be handled this easily by human hands. I thought she enjoyed the little surprised activity because it caught her momentarily off guard and plus it presented her with once again the use of the scientific process to test for facts and not be led by unsupported claims. She mediated on this awhile longer "hard mercury", which led into a special homework assignments for the class.

The high school Physics teacher name was Mr. Hines. I would interrupt Mr. Hines by me blurting out the answers to his written formulas on the blackboard. Sometimes I would know the answers even before he would complete the formula. I also recall him inquiring of using a term I had never heard before, " are you a whiz kid?" he asked, If it was not for his perpetual sincerity, I would have translated that into " what are you, a wise guy?". A whiz kid? I replied. Yeah, back in the early nineteen fifty's without any explanation, there were many gifted kids born in this era. "Are you a whiz kid?" he asked again. No, I replied slowly. He wanted me to accompany him to some after school hours Physic club at Wayne State, I was honored, but I knew somehow this would bring too much attention to me and it would cut into my playtime after school, and we all know how dangerous and fun that could be. Again somehow, I skated past the traditional lines of structure.

Mr. Hines and I discussed complex physics problems. The calculation of energy released during the average rainfall and concluded that it was more energy released than during an atomic blast. The only difference was that the rain's energy was released in smaller increments over longer periods of time versus the atomic explosions, which was released all in a slit second. We even discussed things like nuclear space travel, the many problems facing scientists to make this a reality, I would offer solutions like containing the reactions in a sound proof container only for him to reveal a greater problem, "how would you prevent the reaction from becoming white hot?" he would ask. I knew fool well that this kind of space travel presented all kinds of physical problems and was not the most efficient method of travel anyway. Because all the while, no matter what I did I somehow knew intuitively to keep things I had come to know a close secret. Not to even share my extra curricular activities with the person I admired the most Mr. Hines. I am sure he never knew how I truly felt about him. I would go through Physics class like any other of classes I attended; making friends, like with a girl named Tayna Golden. During every Physics class, we would share a fifty-cent chocolate candy bar. She was way out of my league because she was one of the most popular girls in the school. However, I never thought of her as girlfriend material. Moreover, I was sure that was part of my attraction to her and her being comfortable around me. We remained simply friends for years after High School. I would occasionally run into her at restaurants, basketball games and the like. Our friendship was always just that, distant but always glad to see a friend.

Chapter 15

One would think that if even one of the strange things that happened to me truly happened I would run and tell the world with excitement. There are other realities equally compelling that rise to the surface and instinctively make a person become mute.

Until today, I have told no one of my secret experiences. I have vaguely told my wife mainly to avoid causing alarm, fear and putting her life in imminent danger. Not even a friend, schoolmate, and brother. I have scantily told my mother and one friend Kenny Smith. I have never discussed these events with my sister, church member, absolutely no one until now.

The many struggles with secondMan the "boogieman" had taken a toll on me over the years. I started to get tired of the constant attack and my counter attacks. I am convinced much of my incursions were in conjunction with an invisible host during those times, over the years I had lived in constant fear, because I seemed alone most of the time. I was an inventor on a quest to fight what appears to be an almighty enemy. I was engaging in the creation and destruction of secret devices to fight my nocturnal intruders, my unseen, all-powerful, elusive foe. Unbeknown to me I had developed without noticing the most awesome abilities. I cannot tell if some of my abilities were implanted during some of the strange event such as during the incident that occurred with invisible wind that had my leg flaring in an unseen storm, or if I was in fact born with these extraordinary extra senses. I often wondered if it all started after the astonishing boot-of-clouds event. Or, was I empowered by the mysterious sky down by the river. Perhaps I was modified when that silver object appeared in my right hand during my first encounter into the great descent. During tis particular descent, I was presented a most peculiar question as I stood silent in pitch black darkness from the one known as DayStar, "Are you seeing… are you woke?" He asked.

I did not know if just one or if all of these events contributed in some way to me becoming what I am or were they just revealing what I already was. One thing for sure, this was far different from anything I had developed. My destructive creations it seems, was only a prelude of an unseen thing about what I truly was becoming or what was simply being revealed about my true self.

One of those abilities was the ability to glide. Others things I would find out later had devastating consequences and so too would my adversary the boogieman. Thereafter I practice and grew into my new strengths until one day my lifelong terrorist would himself soon be terrorized.

After much observation and secret experiments that went way beyond known science, I indulged into sciences of the unseen. I became even more advanced with experiments in those days creating devices, testing and then destroying them to keep them hidden from everyone. I mastered the means of mind travel (traveling of mind speed) the mind is itself a conduit allowing the comings and goings of other minds. I have traveled using a much older and physical travel referred to as phasepointing(rational axis of star systems.) Little did I realize that my early childhood insect collection held secrets to understanding the larger universe and the mystery of physical flight. One day while standing in the night just watching the stars I heard these words…

need a bumblebee know why he can fly to fly? A man can indeed fly.

Here are my actual notes from that first experience of spontaneous flight dated May15, 1975.

I have flown, rising clumsily at first, and then rising rapidly under the cloak of the night sky. Panic stricken for this was an unsuspected surprise to me. Rising uncontrollably, crashing into tree branches trying to grab them to stop my rapid accent. Terrified, my arms reached for everything I passed. Later pretending to use my weights for exercise, I secretly inserted them into my specially made clothing on my chest. The extra weight two hundred pounds would slow my ascent. I would press and hold the huge weights to my chest, as I would feel a feeling of levitation coming on that would abruptly lift my body into the air. I would be as high as skyscrapers seeing their rooftops and the twinkling of the night-lights below. Hearing the sounds of the city life, kids playing, cars honking, and sirens far down below.

At first, I was terrified, because this flying ability just came one night without warning. I started small with something like lifting myself one or two feet off the ground for a couple of seconds. There were even times when cars I was driving soared for several seconds gliding several hundred feet. Since then some forty years later, I have mastered all forms of levitation, flight, and in-flight matter-phase. I have had many controlled flights, I have cruised silently and high as the clouds to see distant stars clearly and witness the tiny twinkling of city light below. I can manage levitation so well I have done reverse slow motion rotation yet moving forward in my kitchen not touching a wall and only inches above the floor when I knew no one else was in the house. Absolutely nobody else knew about these test flight navigation. These are the kinds of secrets I have kept all of my life. I have learned how to synchronize my frequency with mind matter passing right through one matter to the next as though it is air rapid flight can be achieved without regard to physical objects. Catching the borealis wave I have I flown long distances. Being familiar with the electronic planetary and galactic cycles coupled with direct mental phase out, I have seen the earth pass beneath me in a blur. However, the most fastest and efficient, but the most dangerous, for one can in an instant see one-galaxy pass and another approach in seconds. If one knew not of the exact fraction of a giga second to change cycles and realign with a new axis, one could find himself hopelessly lost light years away with no hope of ever relocating his point of origin again let alone defragging in empty space or inside a solid object.

After a while, early in my developing dominance, I felt invincible. Many days with my hands on my hips looking at the business of my peer I was feeling indestructible and superior as I watched them do their daily business. I had many lessons from an unknown source, most on the control of anger, the discretion of decisions, teaching me to better love my wife. At this time, I did not know of other infinitely more powerful beings like the TolekAlwa or the mMutota. But I was reminded in one of many insulting lessons that despite one's exoneration one must manage humility. Hear now this one lesson from a voice of a distant orator…

As I stood in my living room harvesting these comparison thoughts, I saw…an bumble bee rising from a field of grass, and as this bee rose I felt it boast even as I boasted of my secret powers of flight… I heard these words …bumble bee…make yourself!

Not to mention chill bumps erupting on my skin. I realized at this point that someone could definitely read my every secret thought and in an instant respond to them. I immediate understood what the message meant. The science of flight is not for birds to boast. I since then learned to study humility. The early years of chasing insects coupled with the distant invisible voice of correction would give many lessons of conduct in self-control. Not only did the boot of clouds allow me to see through their eyes, I was also privy to their code of conduct and counsel as well.

I heard him preaching…

It is not enough to fly high, as one rise… high... his respect for others rights must widen exponentially… so as he rises high… his respect for his fellow beings is a pyramid beneath him. —*Tenakatonon Law*

I understood clearly that neither the bumblebee nor I was the cause of flight, and I best master the skill at hand, no time for brashness or even secret internal private exaltation. Even a grain of sand of boasting, I remember from my fishing lesson, not one thing must be changed if the whole thing might not work.

Though never helping with my fight against my nemeses "the boogieman", the strange-sounding thunder was timely about giving counsel it seems. I began to wonder about this, are they even aware of my boogieman dilemma?

After years of focus came the mastery of flight. With much practice, I could rise from standing casually upright in mid conversation on a city sidewalk to the upper reaches of the sky in minutes. Most notably one evening on a street called

Eight Mile Road, I had owned a garden shop there for several years, after talking to employees late that night and sending them home, under the cover of darkness I rose up and quickly entered the base of clouds. Where as before, I would have wobbled and been fear stricken, I now fly high passing penetrating and exiting the clouds. I descent relocate and match the T-Phase frequencies that they- the boogiemen use to stay veiled from human senses. I saw the huge sky cities of the secondMan—the boogieman had built. This three quarter specie is endemic—living nowhere else outside this immediate solar system. They also populate five invisible moons orbiting the earth. They remained hidden from firstMan—human detection for thousands of years. They reside above the clouds in the skies above. I always sensed there was a vast empire overhead. Now I know for sure because now I see them plainly. Yes, now I could not only see my adversary I discovered a method to covertly reach and invade his heavenly abode in the sky above. There are many functions of an A1, one function as you know is to tell stories or present warnings in the form of a story, and this process is often referred to as "a strange sounding thunder" and another function, secondMan will soon to find out. There will be unseen war in the sky cities above in the hidden realm of earth.

Chapter 16

Finally, I developed the mind grafting technology and mental discipline to infiltrate the boogieman's descent-level. This achievement took years. After many inventive efforts, I was able to occasionally invade their world. Yes, I had managed to appear invisible for a very short amount of time I could avoid detection long enough to slip pass their outer parameter detection sensors right into their main headquarters. Whatever I planned to do, I had only seconds to do it. I found there were many more of them than imagined.

SecondMan is like us, not only similar in building cities but in population expansion, degradation in pleasure and the enslavement of other life forms less powerful then themselves. We like them, survive from utilizing body parts from other specie. Rnkstimno(parasites that pilferage animals and the unborn). They are in the dark sciences of bio scavenging and we are slowly becoming like our loathsome adversary the boogieman. For, we are an indirect by-product of their many nightly insurgences whose missions are to extract our self generating moral substance, essence of life for their own sustenance. They routinely seek out those with a thirdEye and disable it to keep mankind in the dark for thousands of years in the future.

Chapter 17

The River's Sky is Alive:

Earlier I said that many beings move among us unseen. I also said that there were signs that everyone missed, my teachers, friends, family, well I should add myself to the list, because the thing I tell you like all the other things actually happened and yes I missed the meaning of it, I hid and ignored it and forget about it for a long time. I remind you repeatedly at times I did not know then what I know now. The following two incidents I am about to describe occurred about the time when I was desperately searching to construct a method to strike back at the boogieman. Believe me, the civilizations of earth are no match for what I encountered and the things I must do to persevere against such an uncommon adversary as secondMan. When I say I have no fear of normal things. The abnormal things were causing all my heart fluctuations. Such as the sky reacting almost human like to my thoughts!

Okay here it goes; One day as I am driving home from work I was thinking of a certain very private thought. The sky reacted to my thoughts by turning very black and became quite animated. The clouds morphed into infamous cumulus types or which much of the cloud exterior fluctuated rapidly. Not realizing it was my own thoughts that caused all this, I kept thinking until the edges started to descend rapidly to encompass the entire area where I was. It got so dark in seconds I got scared. My thoughts automatically changed, ceased thinking my private thoughts. It was this event, not the boogieman that would actually be one of the scariest things I had witnessed. Think about what I just told you. Put yourself in my shoes, you are a normal person right? The sky gets very angry with you and you know it. Wait, a minute the sky? You must think I am perhaps being symbolic. No I mean just what I said, the sky. I must remind you that I have abilities that let me feel or sense things, the movement of matter, people, boogieman, water, and now an angry sky. Yes, the sky did turn black in mid-day just in that small area covering about one or two miles. What made it worse, this mass of black clouds threatened to start lowering themselves down coming close to the ground. However, I knew it was because of me and this made me so afraid. That fear I experienced that day was different from the fright generated by the boogieman intruder. The cloud sky thing I sensed was angry. It was not the boogieman; it was not the empire in the sky either, what was this? What was that all about? There is more.

For the most part things happen over an extended period. Time has a way of providing what some people call hindsight. In retrospect, I see clearly the path I was on a was very unusual path. Not only was I being exposed to an angry sky, a distant voice of oration, the boogieman, there was the occasional just plain weird thing that would occur.

I later discovered that the incident I was exposed to had intrinsic value of great importance about me and my reality.

Sometime the wind of change will gust into the life of a person—literally blowing his reality away then replacing it with another unseen reality but just as real.

While living in the apartment I would experience the one thing I accredit with giving me a revelation of several truths. If you recall, earlier I said that some thing's that you think is true is in fact a lie, and now I will tell you that some things you've heard that deep down you think is a lie, fairy tales or is just some made up story of some kind that survived over time, this could in fact be true.

If what I tell you next make you kind of nervous it is understandable. You may as well grab a seat and laugh to hide your fear for this one.

One morning my wife headed out to work. On this particular morning, My wife and mother-in-law worked at the same place. After seeing her out the door, I continued watching her from our bedroom window as she made it to her parent's car who was waiting in the parking lot. I could see the top of her head as she passed under our bedroom window. After they drove off, I decided I could catch a few more zzz's before getting ready for work. Therefore, I hopped back in bed and pulled the covers over my head. Slowly at first, I felt something coming from the closet or not so much the closet as from the direction of the entire wall. At first, it started as a small wave then the rhythmic pulses got stronger and stronger. The force of it increased until it felt just like a tidal wave and it was passing right through me! I sought to hold on to something but there was nothing. It felt as though I was being blown and pushed and threatened to be carried away by this invisible but real and very strong wave. I will never forget, although my life did not flash before me, the thought of me dying entered my mind. I was not terrified at this unfolding event until… I decided to open my eyes and see if I could observe what was taking place. I cracked my eyes to a slit, only to catch a glimpse of what I can only describe as horror. I saw my leg, my right leg thrashing and flapping vigorously as a flag being blown by the wind. My leg should have broken based on the way it was moving all on its own. Yet, I did not feel a thing. No pain or movement, nothing! I did not even know my leg was moving until I took a sneak peek. Think about that for a minute. Think about how you would feel if this was actually happening to you. Nothing in life, school or church had prepared me for this strange encounter. My mind was exposed to a force so immense that this thing could just sweep me away like this, as a rapidly moving tidal wave carries trees.

After seeing my right leg from the thigh joint down waving, flapping, thrashing away in all directions being blown leftward by this invisible force—it should have twisted off. Frightening! For the first time I felt my life would surely end this morning. I knew I was going to die. I was going to die! I had never even wrestled with this thought before, not even after many encounters with the boogieman. The force of the wave was getting even stronger. I was thinking about how to prepare myself for death. Thinking quickly, I recall thinking that I did not have much time to prepare. If I must go out….I struggled to think, think, think! It was hard to even think with this going on. I had nothing to cling to, nothing to bring me comfort at this crucial moment. What suddenly entered into my mind was a dream I had several years earlier. In this dream, a man was sitting on a horse in serious dialog with me. The man was trying to get me to remember four items of importance he pointed to that was written in his right hand. He noticed that I was not at all taking him serious. At this point, he stopped trying to teach me. He paused, and in a most serious tone to get my undivided attention, his last words to me was… "Remember the Daystar!" This dream, which had been buried for several years, comes to mind now? In my darkest hour, in this lonely room, I will die repeating the word DayStar! At the time, I did not have a clue to the significance of this word. Upon not being able to speak the words due to the force of the wave, I then thought to utter the word DayStar in my mind as my last thought. I was ready to die. The boogieman had never even crossed my mind this time. This was not the work of the boogieman.

I noticed surprisingly, ever so slightly, just a slight decrease in the force of the wave. "DayStar"! I would mentally repeat again, and I noticed for sure no matter how small, but there was a drop in the force of this energy wave. Getting excited with hope, I recall repeating the word many times until the powerful wave diminished just enough to continue and just pass on through me, without taking or blowing my soul away with it. My leg slowly stopped thrashing about and abruptly flopped on the bed, it was still attached. I lay there now very dumb founded, perhaps in a state of shock. This was indeed some kind of physical force or perhaps metaphysical—mental and physical. But no sooner had I collected my senses back together my scientific instincts kicked in, all I could think of was running across the field to the neighbor that lived directly across from us. They would be in the same path of this energy wave. Isn't that funny? That was my first reaction. But I could not bring myself to do it for now. How would I explain to total strangers what just happened?

The word DayStar given to me in an old dream several years earlier saved my life that morning. Days later, I would rationalize more about the old dream, the man on the horse and this energy wave incident. If this DayStar thing worked so well on the wave… I thought is it possible? …If this worked on the energy wave is it possible that DayStar really exist? Wwhhhat! More importantly, could the DayStar name work on the boogieman!!! Perhaps for the first time in all my life I may have stumbled upon the weapon, the weapon that stopped something more powerful than anything I had felt from all the encounters with the boogieman combined. Is it possible, I thought that I could use it, the name DayStar against the boogieman?

I do clearly recall thinking, if this energy field really exist, and it did, and if the name DayStar really worked when uttered, then, then, this DayStar thing might be as real!

In an indirect way, I possibly discovered something that saved my life, and at the same time through deductive reasoning as called in philosophy, develop an unprecedented realization. A realization buried under lies and time, in a world of corner store myths a real truth. Not a verbal, psychological, blackmail for money word, but a real something or somebody. I'll never forget another consideration that rushed my mind that day… You see in the neighborhood that I grew up in there was always a bully or two. There was this one bully of bullies named Robert King. I had heard of this guy every since kindergarten. Robert King this, Robert King that, all the way until high school. I'll tell you how bad he was, if someone called his name, every one nearby would scatter. Why? Because he is real and his power is real. Just because I had not known or seen him personally in eighteen years did not make him non-existent. I finally meet him but understand me, up to this point he was only a story, a person in a story. From that scenario, I could conclude from what just happened to me, if the wave and the boogieman feared the DayStar, then there must be something or some truth to its existence. Any good scientist would let logic and facts conclude his findings. Ms. Harrison's law was also proving itself to be invaluable, giving support now to what others call myth and deep in the back of my mind even I thought some stories are but a myth. But isn't this whole thing funny, I mean, a tale of a bully confirms the myth of an unseen being? That which seem true though evil, like the bully can be the only fact that gives credence to an unseen myth.

Earlier I mentioned a dream about a man on a horse, who was the man on the horse? It was just a dream wasn't it? What is this DayStar? What does it mean? Perhaps it means nothing to us. But, to those in another reality and who understand symbolism, know to flee.

Yes, that particular morning, indeed an invisible wind has blown, not only did it blow away some of my own mis-guided beliefs, but has also blown in some hope in perhaps helping me solve a life long battle against a most powerful enemy, "the boogieman".

I have attached a written account of the incident the very day it happened. Note the date on the bottom of the page 05.15.78. I was accustomed to jotting and dating things down as a habit. I wrote this and hid it in a Bell and Howell Electronic book that remained under my close observation till this day. Read the notes I made when the actual incident occurred. It varies slightly from the account that I described above by minor details.

Actual notes from over thirty years ago read…

"Lying on side and woke periodically at the time. Half sleep or half woke when I felt it coming from across the room. I tried to move vigorously to elude the paralyzing sensation I thought was coming. Instead there came miraculous wave afar wave or pulses of the semi paralyzed sensation. Notably, I felt the bed end sway and sort of as if it was about to be rolled-up as one would roll a thick blanket. At this point also, I then realized that I was being sensually sustained for the presents of something to someone thing did not want me to move but I was persistent in denying. The pulse felt as though they were pushing my left top leg against my body, trying to force it up against my body or chest. I struggled; my foot pressing against my calf my whole left leg blew and waved an in a strong wind.

I also did not know at the time, but this force was my first encounter with the descent-level relocation energy field. Someone was further exposing my mind to unseen realities that were undetectable to even my thirdEye. “Are you woke?” An invisible voice asked. Over time, I was being slowly awakened. Awakened, but for what purpose?

Chapter 18

Years ago everything invisible thing or person was the boogieman that meant to do me harm. Everything that happened was because of this invisible nemesis. However, over time as I started to piece these enigmatic things together, I slowly began to form a new revolutionary thought. Was this cloudHost somehow connected to what had protected me from harm in the past? The falling bunk bed? Was it connected to the lion in the chair vision I saw as a kid? I began to think further, was it the cloud I witnessed in the devastating attack on the boogieman's strong hold in the sky? Destroying it with clouds of smoke and thick red and nuke white hot lightning? What was this powerful wind? Why did I get help to survive the invisible storm, but no aid in my battles with the boogeman? Who is DayStar? Overtime, some questions were about to be answered, or should I say, some hidden truths unraveled.

By this time in this stage of my life, Robert King, the boogieman, the River's Sky, and "DayStar" are real. Robert King I knew, the boogieman I knew, but who were these other two? The answer is hidden in plain view. I would discover the answer in the clouds.

Chapter 19

I was permitted to see, giant animated rainbows in the night sky, in places and conditions were it is scientifically impossible for a rainbow to exist. I have observed multiple rainbows animate and illuminate the darkness. Colossal in size, often the circumference would arch from earth to our moon. The most spectacular sighting took place one night when a rainbow flickering in multiple duplications of itself, rapidly expanded and arched from horizon to horizon then froze holding this its positon with the moon sitting at the vortex or center of the rainbow highest point, like a great white gleaming pearl on display. The moon glowed as though shinning for the gods that night. It was indeed a spectacular sight. The deities of the lost son's are readying to execute god knows what unknown function against evil.

Here on earth, the rainbow is an ornament that appear after a good summer rain, to other entities and life forms that can see ninety-nine more truth, the rainbow is a mark of destruction, a weapon capable of wielding devastations on a galactic scale. This particular host of beings I witnessed that night, are along way from there point of creation. They prepare to return home soon; but not before their departure, they plan on destroying some resident evil in our mist. These beings I observed that night are an extension group of the true son's of Tenakatonon.

The son's of Tenakatonon are ancient specie. For centuries, they have taken ridicule from their scribes and gained lessons from the orators. The Tenakatonon entity has not so much as crucified one scribe in two hundred million years. Nor has there been a murder over this same span of time.

They have hardened souls. I have seen them and their captains on several occasions. Their chest armor is soot black at the center with black streaks spreading across the surface similar to the blasts marks you see on jet engines.

The Tenakatonon have learned that truth from their scribes, some times constructive hurt prunes a greater soul. They have preserved their entire genetic morality. And the sermons I hear today are from even the greatest and oldest of their scribes, the famed sciatic(the elder of elders) his sermons are repertoires of lessons learned spanning many millenniums. If we think we know love, we experience "but a slice" of what one of the most famed son's feel toward this chief scribe.

The sons have not deviated from years of wisdom. I have learned much from the invisible orator's sermons. The son's are ever testing the ego. In judging the messenger, I almost missed the message once. During one of my early descents, I happened upon three very old hags. They did not look appealing to me at all, kind of repulsive I may add. But, one of three drunken matter fact, the most drunken of the witches actually observing her provided me the key to achieving a technique that could induce a rapid ascent when lifting off to fly without fear. I learn to discard first impressions—an early lesson taught to me from the River's Sky over the years.

Chapter 20

I will now speak of the one being known by several different names. I speak of DayStar as firstMan identifies him, secondMan by those who can perceive him; he's known as archieDominio. From where he originated, he was known as sanwarcharchete(that which arcs – that what unites by fire).

I come to know sanwarcharchete by all three of the names but more importantly, I know sanwarcharchete by symbol. Symbols cannot be mistaken nor misunderstood. Let me now tell you of the dreaded and most unfortunate event I seen that took place over four hundred years ago. First, it is no need to tell you of the exact place because it is of such an inconceivable distance and location. Television here has underestimated the true width of space. In reality, if you traveled forty thousand years at light speed, you would have only reached the next closest galaxy called Alpha Centari. Physical travel also presents another dilemma not addressed in television movies, that is, the ten thousand years required to slow down your spacecraft to avoid over shooting the target galaxy. So as you can now clerly see, physical space travel is not very efficient. No, physical travel is not the means of traveling great distances amonst more advanced specie. There are other kinds of travel involving matter and mind, atomic rotation, and orbital phasemations. Then, there are dimensions, but known to other specie as descent-level relocation. There are infinite levels occupying one space. In fact, this is how different beings remain both near and yet so far or separated and undetectable from one another. So, I will speak to you of doors opening and moving from floor to floor like in an elevator—utilizing this method is what allowed me to achieve my first invasion into the boogieman's invisible empire that was located on the furthest ring of the sixth outer moon.

At this point in the story …you now know of firstMan--us, secondMan "the boogieman", and somewhat of the son's of Tenakatonon, and the mMutota, there is a fourth entity I briefly mentioned earlier… sanwhachechetel. Let me supply a little more detail about this being(s). As stated before, he is pivotal in how things came to be and how things will end.

The mMutota specie was never meant to occupy physical space. But, they will transform to occupy it in an instance, if they knew sanwhachechetel resided here on the fourth descent-level of physical matter.

Their most awesome military arm, the mMutota-cu would one day trans-descent to physical space in search of sanwhachechetel. There are those in this universe the mMutota-muucutu, who are on a mission to locate Sanwacachetal, also known by several other titles or names ArchieDomino or as DayStar and to others FallingSun.

ArchieDomino has reestablished ecuomiomin (law of house) to his consciousness. He has secretly remained hidden here on earth for the past several hundred years. He recently dispersed his own one of a kind encrypted mark emanating into time and space; what we scientists here interpret as sunspots. This action on previous occasions has created mysterious disturbances, causing compasses to whirl, time warps, gray walls, eye of the hurricane, and mental disorientations. Several days ago, ArchieDominio dispersed the last of the symbolic emanations.

These last dispersions has been recognized not only by the son's but even the dreaded mMutota-cu. FallingStar's exact layer, dimension, and physical presents is now known. Further, more, it confirms the mMutota suspicions over the past several hundred years, that he ArchieDomino is still in fact alive. He did survive? Now the question, will his own mMutota faction or the dreaded mMutota muuctu military extension having also decrypted the signal reach the source of origin first? FallingStar himself will plan to return to seek those who attacked him ages years ago. Had he died or been destroyed from such a unprecedented attack from the muucutu branch, sanwarcharcetel would have been the first ever of a mMutota to perish in a act of war. If I could, I would even warn them the muucutu mMutota branch, because they have no idea what he FallingSun has become over the past four hundred years. Benevolent yes? Armed yes; the universe of many descent-levels will learn the true purpose and power of the rainbow wielding entity has become over the past several hundred years.

I saw sanwacarchetel's story unfold before my very eyes on evening… Seeing through the eyes of the tanakanoton I witnessed an event that took place several hundred years earlier.

One day as I sat in front of the fireplace, my back warmed by its flickering flames, sitting motionless, staring, I began to hear… and through my right eye I began to see my mind zoomed to an event that unfolded over hundreds of years earlier.

Chapter 21

Enter, (Domino, Domino, Domino) FallingSun:

Originally residing on several descent-levels above our own existence, there exist the sons of Tenakatonon hosts. Sanwacarchetel's is a former archterDoingo(might of arms) of a great military host of the tenakotonon. Sanwacarchetel was traveling a path he had taken many times before after hearing one ofs the invigorating sermons messaged to all from the great nazauscolt orator. He meditated as he traveled, reflecting, alone, alone he insisted himself for there was nothing a mMutota had to fear ever. They are at the top of the evolution chain of humanoid species. He often traveled on the outer edge of creation. But on this day there would be an unprecedented act committed by the dreaded dacato (lesser by power) sons of mMutota-do. They would hope to ambush sanwacarchetel and remove his mind matter conversion helmet for the enhancement of their own relocation transfer technology.

As sanwacarchetel enjoyed his stellar cruise he phased in to a walk, taking physical form on a dash –T frequency(seventh descent-level) thus cloaking him from all-seeing mammals so as not to disturb the serene environment. His silhouette slowly emerged over several small hills and burst into a thousand shadows and long extended entrance of the host above created stretched cloud formations. He was between two mountainous knolls deep in the valley when the unthinkable happened…

mMutota-muucu troops silently materialized pouring over the hills ridge with weapons already blazing ga-zillions of rain like pins of firepower. The sudden firepower bombarded sanwacarchetel's lower body–shields holding, but the weapons blast slightly forced him off-balance. Within a split second, more weaponry unleashed, mixing in with the rain of golden pins already hitting their intended taerget. This heavier firepower consisted of bluish balls of arc-matter by the thousands. These blast were aimed at his legs and midsection with attempt to destroy the energy shields – sanwacarchetel broke into a run; shields weakening. The garrison of attackers pursued firing a continuous and blinding barrage of twirling golden cigar glowing mass-disrupters by an uncountable number. Pin like raining matterstramers, blue hallow arc matter, and golden matter-disrupters all at once toward one target. They closed in he felt fear for the first time in his life. Sanwacarchetel attacked with a force reserved for entire fleets of armed destroyers. Now sensing the troops reading his mind, every thought to escape was useless, they closed in still firing, he ran slower and slower… even when he thought to escape by opening a dim phase descent-level sub portal, the attackers responded with more aggression with an increased firepower intensity that created blindness to the surrounding area. Still sanwacarchetel strategized… I will send a fake thought of giving up and slump to the ground, then just as quick, jump for the dim phase door opening at his left side. Again, the Mutota read his mind and immediately responded with the intensified firepower of many thunders never letting up. They quickly closed rank on sanwacarchetel as he lunged with his shields failing; he felt the fiery pins by the millions, the blue acs thumping and burning, and the golden glows knocking him a small distance now with each hit, his consciousness was no more. The areas whiten with the continuously weapons fire, Then, slowly the thunderous echoes became silence.

After all firing had ceased and the weapons glow had diminished, sanwacarchetel's body was nowhere to be seen. The mMutota are perplexed as they check for residuals on microscopic levels. They have never seen anyone withstand such firepower. Was their target incinerated they thought? The commander's immediately summoned millions of scanners and matter detectors. No trace element of sanwacharchetel was detected. They searched for over four hundred years and still are not convinced that sanwacarchetel was destroyed Yet they must believe that nothing not even the sons could have survived the firepower unleashed during that dreaded attack. This attack was committed by the macta-muucu(Overlords of the outer edge of the realm), truth be told, now that I know them-the mMutota and the extent of their technology, nothing ordinary could have survived that attack.

Through the white-hot blinding firepower, in my right eye, I saw a portal door zoom open in multiple concentric ripples and the sun fall from it. From this side of the universe, a legend began.

Enter FallingSun

A gigantic portal hole that maintained travel between two descent-levels for several seconds would introduce a new entity into physical space that would help alter evil in a all blinded world of humans. A few other people with a thirdEye witnessed this historic event noting that a dim lit sun was seen falling from the dark sky to the ground, it was raining hard that night.

Far back in the deep in the south of Thomason Alabama a defenseless unarmed family was escaping from a posse of armed slave traders that night. Running for their lives, they slip and fell repeatedly as they splash and ran in wet mud. The pregnant wife, the husband carrying another baby girl about two years old, tightly held the baby to his chest as he ran. Their young boy hung to the pant leg of his farther as he struggled to keep up. They could hear the sounds of horse hoofs upon the ground, the shouting of angry men, and the barking of dogs closing in. Hunting people captured and branded as slaves is the clearest indication of the presents of evil in its purest form. It also confirms that that particular society is void of true religion and that its citizens are impotent. This particular posse of human hunters were responsible for a resident of the secret Underground Railroad being murdered because for their helping this small runaway family to avoid capture early in the week. In the pouring rain, the faces of terror stricken family of five were momentarily revealed as the lightning flashed and the thunder roared. The wife's tears mixed with the down pouring rain. The wife, daughter, little boy and the newborn was suddenly instructed by the farther to take refuge in a barn just up ahead, they did—he was all to familiar with what these types of American flag waving bible thumping patriots do to women and little under age girls after the they catch, mutilate then kill the husbands.

As the mother and children ran ahead, the farther turned in a different direction, he ran for short distance and took refuge next to a huge line of thick shrubbery. Maneuvering and timing his actions making sure he was intentionally spotted by one of the posse riding horse back close behind—who's large rain-soaked hat was rapidly bouncing as rain poured down onto his angry face from its crevices.

After the posse pack-leader caught up to the farther he yelled to him… "I see whit ya dun did back their, its worthy, mighty worthy!" Referring to the farther sacrificing himself for the safety of his wife and kids. Then pulling out his whip, the pak-leader began to beat the farther further complimenting him, "But in thi name uf gud almity I must git yurns back fur my day's pay!". The very first swing of the wip the farther quickly grabbed, wrapped it around his wrist, yanked the man from off his horse. Then choked him to death with his own whip as both struggled in the slippery mud. Others of the posse-pack on horse back were not far behind, they all rushed in at once, ganging up and began beating the farther. He managed to kill several more of them with his bare hands disarming and using their own weapons against them before they eventually observe him fall to the ground. But the posse-pack discovered all to late that falling to the ground was a defensive ploy. The hunted man would use his legs to sweep several of them to the ground and at the same time killing them and slashing some of the dogs with his knife with lightning speed. Still, thirty or so more reinforcements arrived, rushing in to help eventually subdue this most troublesome and angry man. These are the kinds of slaves that American society most feared, these were the ones labeled as evil and sought to be identify and killed at an early age. This slave, always playing the role of the humble servant, managed to go undetected and eluded them for years.

Chapter 22

One group of posse-pack continued onward straight ahead in pursuit of the mother and her children. In the meantime, another pack of vicious bounty hunters stumbled upon someone else, something else that looked to them like a larger than usual slave. Black, very black, blue black lying face down in the mud with a skull-cap looking helmet made of bluish gold metal formed tightly to his odd shaped head. Unknown to them, this would be the last human hunt they and many others like them would enjoy in the name of gud almity, duty and cun-try.

Immediately the slave hunters did what any civilized slave hunter would do if seeing a black human being lying in the mud, they began to flog, vehemently beat with their whips and hurl verbal insults at him. All their efforts of kicking and stomping seemingly had no effect on the person, as he lay motionless in the rain-drenched mud. Their physical assaults return the noise of solid thumps, sounding as though they were hitting hardened metal as opposed to human flesh.

Due to the loud commotion and vicious beating being delivered to the host member of the archieDominio began to slowly awaken. Though severely injured from the mMutota assault several nights before, he began standing totally unaffected by the physical attack being inflicted upon him. His head gear glowing with faint reactivation circuitry. The wild posse repeatedly strike and kick at him escalating their physical attack, he continued to slowly rise. Now hovering several inches above the ground, the dogs once growling and biting yelped, backing up and took to running. The slave hunters all stood staring up to see the man in the mud now seem to be a giant statue rising, rising with a massive rainbow first emanating from his shoulders. Then in a several flashes of red lightning expand from his shoulders to the gathering black clouds overhead. A strange-sounding thunder, started to erupt and echo across the country side that night. What the flashes of plasma lighting revealed this time was another kind of terror seen this time in the eyes of slave hunters. They, in the name of gud, stood spell bounded, literally "shaking in their boots."

Calling on the name of their slave drenching in blood gud would not answer and help them this dreadful night. Their gud was perhaps experiencing the same terror as they. The eLattice technology expands Archienatus to enormous size, his eForce—bio defense circuits now fully activated. Then the embattled alien host went into self-defense and protective first function mode. First, silentReconSentinels and TEU-Threat Elimination Units dispersed in a three-sixty, three axis radius. These TEU assume a corporeal appearance in the form of giant orbs of plasma lightning. The purpose of their deployment is to identify and eliminate any advancing aggression—these orbs were dispatched by the hundreds. The TEU silentReconSentinels concentrically spreaded out systematically disposing of all whom they came in contact with. Add to this violent re-awakening and the recent destruction of the mMutota forces just several days earlier, the TEU's were still antagonized. After the first pass, the orbs began another recon run with even more vengeance than the first. Rapidly re-scanning all the bio organisms in the area for any sign of thoughts of aggression. There was this strange sounding thunder as the TEU's found and executed their targets.

Wild posse men, whom human hunters who run in packs and attack the innocent, are now themselves screaming, some dying from shear terror fearing that the wrath of God himself was upon them. A great many were rendered immobile; paralyzed falling to the ground by the TEU mindDisrupters. as the Archienatus was injured and not in full control of his hostActions, the defensive technology self activated in response to the mMutota attackers he had just escaped.

Tens of thousands of confederate and union soldiers were scanned, judged, and dispersed by this second TEU action. Any acts of aggression detected in your memory would have meant your immediate destruction. Distant witnesses described seeing a rainbow high as the clouds, animating its wonderful colors in the night sky and somehow causing great harm. The sky erupted into what seemed like continuous liquid flowing lightning producing the strangest sounding thunder ever heard echoing for miles. His protective bioShpere was of vast size and he-Archienatus rose to the upper region of its zenith in the air high above the ground. As waves of liquid lightning found their targets, the impact of each thunderous blast of annihilation generated winds that made the tree tops wave as water and many of them just snapped flying across the sky.

After a while, the thundering and lightning started to subside. Many of the hosts silentReconSentinels would appear from thin air as they returned from missions of aggressive elimination on all known descent-levels. As they would pass over the slave father and his family, now huddled close together. They too were once again rescanned and was spared because they posses no first thoughts of aggression. However, had the devoted farther even once upon a time in his past hit his wife, the TEU's would have detected it in his mind and he too would have perished that night along with thousands of others.

Normally judgment is neither that severe nor strict, but the silentReconSentinels s was angry and sought every reason to disassemble any thing in their path. It was clear the lightning was under mind control of Achienatus although no visibly signs of commands were being given. Giant lightning T3-orbs lingered above his head, many smaller plasmatic T2-orbs orbited the larger ones. As Archietus looked from the east then to the west so did the many small lightning-orbits preëmpt to follow in the directions he looked. As he glanced side to side emitted preëmptive energy bursts that faded a few feet with his slightness move. The orbiting silentReconSentinels s are self-functioning bioLive detection hostUnits, they upon confirmation by scanning summon the presents of the plasma. Their maneuvers replicated that of dragonflies as they circled their wounded commander. Other giant silentReconSentinels s after executing their eNetic code were phased back into this invisible host returning to anitonon(hostMatter). There was much activity that night, numerous TEU silentReconSentinels s approaching and returning from many directions.

One very angry and aggressive TEU approached rapidly from a direction behind the little girl as she slowly walked toward her farther still laying in the mud, huddled with his family. Trees bending as the TEU swiftly moved forward, the ground glowing from its plasma glow, arcs of lighting annihilating unseen foes, this unit was eliminating every thing in its path on every dimension, this unit was damaged, as it hovered overhead she too was briefly scanned again. Her soaked dirty dress blown by the strong wind created by the approaching TEU behind her, unaware of this danger, she remained staring at the awesome Achienatus kneeling before her. This damaged orb was about to disassemble the innocent little girl also.

Orbs, function as independent decision ingrams, only questionable verdicts are sent back to the consciousness of archemisasus via the mindMatter Interface helmet he wear's on his head for final confirmation or verdict. In extreme instances all mental profiles that fit the aggression outline are automatically eliminated by the TEU's. This careful routine is the only condition that execution is permitted under the son's of Tenakatonon law. The TEU sentinels relentlessly, scanning and re-scanned the frightened people in that area. Until zero aggression is detected the TEU_silentReconSentinels s will remains in the area and in full battle readiness mode. The TEU_silentReconSentinels of Achietus not only eradicated aggression in this physical realm, but on multiple dimensions-descent-levels detecting and scanning even the legions of rectmnca-secondMan who also suffered heavy losses that night from the force and might of fallenSun. "Rainbow of death" as many would refer to this as the night of destruction.

This unprecedented event caused such a turmoil to those living in the sky cities and six moons above because this was their first encounter with a superior being. secondMan like the mMutota, thought themselves to be at the top of the evolution scale. They, like others had their first encounter with a Tenakatonon host.

As the immediate threats to Archiematus were eliminated, his battle shield reduced its intensity. His defense mode self de-activated, the smaller orbiting balls of lightings that swirled slowly high about his head with three sequential rapid bass-like sounds and vibrations collapsed into the bluish sphere, also the rainbow of destruction though never emitting its lethal death emissions it to collapse about his huge shoulders. The remaining larger plasma globes raining down arcs of blinding plasma after hovering in the sky dissipated into the bluish sphere, still weary, half conscious, he, thinking himself to have just eliminated his mMutota attackers. Weary, he slowly kneeled one knee to the ground, nearby houses shook and rattled. Head bowed, and just in a knick of time with his last conscious thought he summoned the last Orb hovering over the small innocent girl back to the host; sparing her from an unjust fate. In that same instant the eViroSimlulator (simulating the physical matter around him) activated to camouflage his presents. Brief winds erupted, while rendering himself invisible to the small band of witnesses. This action would place Archietus into a long hybernation of many years. What he did not know at that venerable time, was that the eDoor had transported him light years and many descent-levels- layers from his home worlds far from his assassins and that he had in fact just destroyed the unsuspecting life forms here, human, reticnia, andw, ieeir0, the neiew, insects, and mammals alike. This unprecedented activity all took place for the first time in existence on the forth decent-level, the physical level in a far way place call earth.

When he would later awake and fully recover, he will find himself burdened with the horrific act he had committed that dreaded night, he will seek to right the wrongs, and be faced with a humanitarian choir to uplift this people in this new place. He will also be faced with a technological choir to re-contact his fellow hosts who cannot believe him destroyed; but none the less, with all their technology and superior intellect, cannot locate him. When awakened, he will find himself surrounded in a world that is more like the mMutota but without the mMutota value system for self-preservation. For the materiaCannaba(animal bite the animal). Or in other words, he'll see a "dog eat dog" world. For, even the mMutota will not kill their own as men of earth do for monetary gain. In the Tenakatonon Archives, Earth will become known as the most horrific place in all civilized existence.

And to those observing from a great distances even the rectenaons(rulers of this realm) witnessing strange great orbs of fire like many suns arc incinerate many seen and unseen foes, and from their viewpoint it was truly judgment day. The destruction that night was upon much specie on many waters, for the matter that your mind is made is to the son's physical matter and real actions. The dragonfly like orb discharge blue-black lightning that rain to the earth. A few people born with the "thirdeye" were not blinded and gave full account of the events. The rainbow animating between the two largest plasma orbs illuminated the night sky. They described what they have witnessed as the "wrath of the gods".

Weeks before many nearby observers claim that they saw the sun fall from the sky as it appears to be at war with other suns that fell with it. This was the mMutota-muucu that made it through the eDoor with aniDomino, there was a great war in the skies but all the mMutota-muucu were destroyed before they hit the ground. Not every one could see this confrontation because it was on a T1-frequency(sixth descent-level.) What some people had witnessed that night, what they took to be a falling star, was in fact the arriving of aniDomino (FallingSun).

Meanwhile on the other side in AnioDomino own descent-level, other hostDomino rushed in to the aide of the fallenStar, they had even started to arrive to this obscure and faraway descent-level, one Domino hostMember in particular is named KemitNonno—meaning he who watches.

For this family of run away slaves, it was a night of terror, jubilation, and unbelievable events. This story they could not bring themselves to retell until many days had pasted. Nothing or no one before this day has ever dared a direct look into the eyes of an angry aniDomino. Only the small girl who crawled out from the barn stood, watched, and yet was not afraid of the horror being rained upon evil by this branch of the son's of Tenakkatonon know them as archtera (blue sabers or blue suns). There are various classifications of aniDomino, some are judge, and some are judge and jury, and then some are the tribunal themselves.

When he does regain full consciousness, I tell you, I have seen what they are capable of, man and the derectinathma(secondMan) will need find a real God to survive a fully functional archtera diDron. For, Judge, Jury, and Executioner will re-awakened among them.

But, this retaliation against the mMutota-cuu, does indeed mark a diversion from the sermons he originally heard and abided. Among the true son's of Tenakkatonon , revenge is replaced with magnanimity. However, this anioDomino is not functioning in accordance with the inherent unkiomene law as his first function. Anguish untold to those who are affixed in his mind, and to those in proximity of the unleashing of the gammatic rainbow. For this gammaDomino will unleash a force nothing can withstand, not even secondMan or a mMutota military legion-they could not withstand an attack from even a wounded archieDomionHost as they later discovered. Wounded yes!

But, that was over four hundred years ago, this is now, he arhieantus, has slowly repaired himself. Worse, due to heavy damage he sustained from the mMutota assault it's currently functioning outside of tanakatonon law. That law we will all discover is Tenakkatonon law and it is what has kept the universe some what orderly till this point.

Unknown to me, this four hundred year old tragedy of this "Anio Domino" or DayStar would later become intertwined my own life.

Chapter 23

I still was about to discover another reality, the reality that just because one does not believe, does not mean imaginary things are not real.

The Descent…

Before I tested my new descent mechanism, surrounding me were four solid bedroom walls. Securing my helmet and activating the mindMerge to Matter device, there was total darkness. After several seemingly excruciating minutes I cautiously, slowly stretched out my hand to feel for the wall that should have been right in front of me and nothing was there!!! After my hand did not register the wall a dispatch of my sensing orbs confirmed that infinity was all around. Breakthrough! The first descent, I have entered the domain of the boogieman.

It took more than several decades for the inexorable process of mindtoMedium(MMI) technology to be perfected or become reliably operative. The technology is highly capable of transferring the human consciousness from one place to another instantaneously. I know this is very different from physical point-to-point travel using horse, airplanes and crude spacecraft of which I remain fascinated. I will attempt to explain how the devre-aLa(medium concealed reality) works. Universal law functions to conceal the mediums of realities from one another.

Water is a different medium than air, and air and different medium than outer space. Sometimes however, different life forms or beings might haphazardly enter the others medium or environment. Using scuba diving gear one can inter the medium of fish for an extended period of time. The mind is also a medium. Mind-Matter falls into the mental mobility variable of medium reality (MMI). Each mind is vastly different in temperament and predictable stability. How many times have you heard family members or friends talk of briefly encountering strange things, like seeing someone or seeing a ghost. The ghosts you see that others cannot, has matched T-frequencies or descent of that person's mind.

There are different kinds of beings occupying the same one place in time, who live in the same environment but are separated by different mediums. One can vibrate into other descent-levels.

There are beings that can transverse many different mediums. From water to land, land to air and air to space and space to mind-matter and mind-matter to time-water at will and respectfully remain undetected, to such, is the sons of Tenakkatonon .

It is with this form of technology that I am able to make my descents. Using this form, another persons mind becomes my temporary reality, my conduit to still another mind. I pass many in the night while you lay sleep. It is the best time to descent travel because the mind is calm and its surface can not easily be thrown into emotional flux. The mind is a constant. It is a medium that is spread to the far reaches of the universe. This form of medium is the common denominator of infinity. In this form, I am instantly in a place even if it were light years distance. I relocate or travel by a process known by a few in the galaxy as descent-level relocation (DLR). But this method of travel has to do with, as much technology as it does with the management of emotion, hence is why firstMan in his natural state has not mastered it and it seems only rectinaStar the great saber-tooth symbol of secondMan and myself utilizing MediumMatter Interface technology are capable.

It was in one of my descent excursions I accidentally descended into the domain of an awesome being. Known to some as rectinalStar and to others as the great sphinx. He has established his symbol over the eons to earthlings as the moon.

Chapter 24

I would use my new created descent-relocator to journey further into the domain of fear.

I remembered the invisible but awesome wave of energy that almost sweep me body and mind away years earlier, if you recall I described this leg bending mind blowing incident to you earlier. I slowly allowed myself to begin to believe the things that happened, really happened. I decided reluctantly to cross back and rethink the invitations from unseen hosts. I restudied my enemy and his power. I again and again contemplated about the wave and the silver thing that appeared from no where I held in my right hand that fearful day when facing the sabertooth ractnalStar—I will tell you of this most awesome encounter shortly. I would begin to slowly to analyze and accept the strange things that defined my life over the years. How reluctant. Even at this writing, I still had a small sense of shame and denial about my life.

But I am in deep waters now, I am allowing my mind to embrace things I have long denied and fought, unseen things, cryptic symbols, beings, a reality I am meant to share yet inwardly tremble every time the thought of going deeper into a descent enters my mind. I remembered a dream about the fish with a man's eye; the fish warned me that it was near time for me to "step out into the deep waters." I will acquaint you more with this fish in the following pages ahead also.

In one of my many descent explorations, I would stumble upon a most fearsome beast.

Chapter 25

At times I have alluded to a symbol of a great and powerful saber tooth tiger, you must remember many things you perceive with the physical eye is only a facsimile or depiction of another hidden being, his personality or the strength of his empire. I speak now with caution, why? The true power of the moon is not known. Though I am a terror, prudence is my partner in an unpredictable universe. I with so much caution avoid creating anger in enemy. Here is the story.

I use to like traveling and exploring the immediate solar system. It is teaming with various life forms and profusion. Many symbols represent placid and docile beings. One can explore for years without ever experiencing aggression of any kind. Many life forms are just as curious as I was about seeing them for the first time, but no aggression was ever displayed from me during any of my chance encounters. In my early incursions I would arm myself when aliens quickly approached, but just as quickly disarm understanding they are only signaling me of my trespassing into their private space.

During this descent into the unknown I had no weapons, no shields of any kind, and I traveled alone. Many times i would find a nice place and take a long walk. This place was peaceful and undisturbed. I walked right upon a huge two hundred foot high, beige looking, mangy covered, saber tooth tiger. He was a muscular beast! He was sitting about a hundred feet ahead off to my right. Silently and motionless he was watching me approach, I felt I had startled him but he was much to seasoned to reveal his presence due to a small un suspecting surprise. He played out his opportunity to remain undetected, he sat motionless. He was huge; his upper half of his body from the midsection and shoulders to the top of his back and head was clearly visible over the top of the large trees I was approaching. At first, I had sensed no feelings from him; I know of other similar creatures similar to this one and yet pose no threat. All of a sudden, I sensed that he knew who I was, and he was filled with immense anticipation of the imminent encountered, and had all the more delight to let me get close so he could strike. Funny, immediately after sensing his aggression, I was feeling the exact same thing—I desperately wanted to get close so as to inflict as much harm as possible. I kept a steady pace in my walk, in the same direction that would take me right past his left side; he would be sitting on my right. By this time in my life, I had no fear of anything, the bigger and meaner the better. I approached with inner great anticipation never looking his way pretending that I did not see him. I mentally detected his great anticipation as well, here we both were about to come face to face with one another—two legends meet. The odds were all in his favor, he was a huge, strong, muscular, claws, and long saber tooth. Plus, he had the element of surprise—so he thought. Coming before him was an unarmed man. However, as we both got closer to one another, both our anticipations started to show, for my walk toward him was more brisk and his head had started to lean in my direction ever so slightly. Nevertheless, he held his stature. I held my pace. My desire to get close to him was uncontainable for I began to know who he was, and whom this symbol represents. I got closer and more and more anxious, his head leaned further downward in my directions as I was about to enter the area close to where his paws extended. I still remember how enormous he was, his body and head extend above the trees. Still without moving his body I see his big brown eye start to keep me in focus as I came ever closer to him, he tilted and leaned his head as I approached closer…his giant head ready, jaws and giant fangs. We both could no longer wait to charge one another. In a flash of an instant, his head came down over top the trees smashing some of them into splinters as he prepared to inhale his seemingly unsuspecting victim. I quickly jumped back, his large head and fangs crashed into the ground, trees branches flew into the air and crashed all around. After my quick jump back, I charged forward and he was now up on all four paws. His huge claws tore the ground in pieces, the chunks of dirt excavated by his claws flung into the air, the ground shook as trembled at his charge attempts. Though fearless, I knew this was indeed a great and mighty beast as mighty as any that I had ever encountered. We repeatedly tore toward one another at break neck speed. The ground trembled as he charged stomping rapidly toward me, with his fierce face and roaring snarl, dirt and trees flying everywhere. For no clear reason I started to draw back my hand as though I had a weapon, I remember this well, I drew back to the ground, and began to bring it forward as we got into inches of each other. I swung at him with all my might, as he prepared another monstrous snap I flung, he snapped. His giant fangs clashed with the force of a great wind.

Abruptly we were being separated, by a widening of space between us? This was strange because it came from seemingly nowhere. As we were being separated, we still gained physical ground as we continued charging each other. This peculiar event happened several times, as we desperately tried to make contact. I realized that we were not alone after all. Out of the corner of my eye I saw four men busy doing something. It was this something that caused the mysterious gorge to appear between the beast and I. The four man crew would align themselves into position, the earth beneath our feet would move backwards. When the crew breaks that alignment, the beast and I would again gain real ground when charging toward one another. I don't know if the beast could see them. However, I sure did. During all the thunderous and deafening noise, I noticed also for the second time that there was without a doubt something in my right hand. It was silver in the shape of a "C". It is this that I through some hidden unknown instinct was going to kill the beast with. I always knew if I could just get to him, I could kill him.

Finally, the crew of mysterious men separated us both for good; the scene became quite and back to normal, but the once beautiful place was a wreck of fallen smashed trees, gorged earth littered with hills of forest debris and dirt.

This was not the being himself but his symbol. I now knew it was a mighty thing. This is the second time I witnessed something trying to open my eyes to the scope of this hidden persons true power. In addition, the mysterious thing in my right hand that appeared, this was powerful enough to slay that beast. I do not think the best knew that or maybe he did, but like me he is fearless to the point of facing one's foe against all odds. If this were the case, by this I know assure that my adversary cannot be easily defeated. For like me he has no regarded for that which he disdain.

What of the four mysterious men? Or what seemed like very ordinary men. During the confrontation with the beast, I recall them transferring the thought of "janitor" to my mind. I also noticed they did not appear powerful at all like other military types of the cloud hosts I have seen. How did they transfer the descent layers, and why did they interfere?

They also are on an undetectable layer that I apparently could not perceive. These questions moving within my mind needed to be answered. I would later find that they, the hidden invisible men were not total strangers to me.

Someone or something else that I could not detect nor sense was always close by. I started to ponder thoughts. I began to think that I might be a part of something else. Something or someone else was certainly making themselves a part of my life. They remained hidden on an invisible descent-level and purposely made it a point to conceal their presents from my detection.

Soon another life-threatening event would again reveal their concealed presence. But, this event would take place here on physical earth at a day camp where I once worked. It was these multiple and many seemingly strange scattered events that eventually made me draw them with the silver thread of truth, bringing them together to reach a startling conclusion, a conclusion that would eventually transcend them these once totally invisible beings boldly to my presents.

Chapter 26

Often now, as I am motivated to quickly finish this story. I see them standing around me as I sit in my chair—several giants surrounding the chair looking down. As I get up and go to the kitchen, another smaller creature is in the hallway that leads to the bathroom. Because now I can since mostly all dimensions and matter, I am aware of their presence. As I make my way back from the kitchen there are none, as I sit a start to write again they return in the kitchen and hallway just outside my room. There is a giant symbol outside my bedroom window, the size of a large building; it is the symbol of a dark lion. It rests in a poised sphinx position. It has positioned un-intimidating across the street facing my house. Outside the family room window, I sometimes see another giant symbol in the form of a resting but vigilant beast. It too resembles a lion or fat bear. As I make my way from the kitchen back to the room I sit and start to write again these invisible sentinels return to stand guard in the kitchen and hallway just outside my room suspended mid-way between floors—thus only the upper half of their bodies extend above floor level. However, they have always been around. I just never could see them before.

I left and reentered the room. As I entered the room to continue writing this time a lolipotfurra(a furry mammal that looks like a dog) sat in my chair facing my computer, as though he understood what was on the screen. Startled at my sudden entrance coupled with the fact that I could see it, it flash away just as fast as light so fast that I would almost second guess that I just seen anything at all. I just sat down in my chair and continued writing. Yes, there are animals in the universe if you want to call them animals. This lopcatillia is more human compassion and genuine concern inside than first and secondMan. He is a good symbol. For what he represents, there is pleasure in what I am doing. He need not flash and scurry away like that. It is as though we can still catch some beings in the other reality off guard, by surprise. I had wished he had stayed. I could pretend all the while that I did not even see him. It had been nearly twenty years since my mother's death I last time I felt one like him.

One night I spent the night alone in my mother's house; I was very sad that she had died. But I've seen things that have died still be alive on another mMatter level. Take my mother's dog named Tippy for instance. I must tell you that Tippy had died a couple of months before my mothers passing. I lay on her living room floor when I mentally detected Tippy in the room. Tippy slowly pretended to go upstairs only waiting for my signal to come and play. So he did only in this instance it was not the physical matter of Tippy instead it was her mMatter. I could see and sense her and she knew it. She came running down the stairs excited and breathing heavily into my face as I continued lying on the floor. Tippy reacted though I hadn't seen her for a long time. Strange huh? So many bizarre incidents. I told you earlier there were hundreds of strange things happening in my life on regular basis.   This particular lopcatillia creature, reminded me of Tippy.

Chapter 27

Each separate and strange episode alone was nothing but something strange. Over a period, these incidents would start to accumulate as evidence —evidence concluding the existence of an unseen presents of an unseen reality mixed in and around our own but going totally undetected from the normal human eye. Not all those that what have so called died has ceased to exist.

As I grew older I would make council with the unseen, my understanding would go beyond my own fears. Before certain one's are allowed into such esoteric knowledge, they spend life times molding the mind, de-programming certain conduct. They do this in hidden ways, subtle ways even using simple things like fishing and insect collecting. Like them, I'm sharing with you all these incidents and stories for a reason.

Chapter 28

Innocent childhood experiences sometimes happen for a future purpose.

I if I tell you that I still go to the river you will think it's due to sentiment. However, what if I told you that I have gone down to the river and on some one or something talked to me from the sky. Yes, someone audibly expressed themselves to me…"down by the river".

The River and I, have a parental to child relationship. During troubling times in my life, I would get a strong inclination to "go down by the river". It is during such burdensome times I would go to pay a visit, to a place that responds to my state of mind. The cloudHosts response many time were quite the opposite of my immediate needs. It seems contrary and totally unconcerned about my wishes and more adamant about my misconception of what it wanted to share. The River's Sky has the social etiquette of rudeness. It is very direct and will get straight to a point. It will blast furnace the ego even during my most contrite or broken state of personal hurt. It holds many of my own secrets. It is one of the reason's I was and what I have become. It knows my secret and most private of thoughts. It knows things I have never ever shared with another person. One day the River's Sky responded to my deep turmoil; what I thought was private, it brought it to the forefront of my mind and slung it into my face giving me a full dissertation of the subject matter with quite disdain I might add.

At the beginning, for over twenty or so years the river

never made itself known. Nothing strange ever happened down there. I just always enjoyed being down by the river watching the waves hearing the sound of the water, seagulls squawking.

The River and the Sky is not what it seems. The river itself is a symbol. A symbol of the existence of man, the materiaManseia(Where the river flows). You will learn of the true meaning of this symbol "of rivers I mean", and again like so many other things afterwards, you will never upon rivers the same.

It was not so much the water down at the river as I would find out later in life as it was the River's Sky. Early in my childhood on two separate occasions, I would see with my own eyes right there in my bedroom two what I come to know now as symbols; but at that time, I saw them only as a "boogieman" which was the first symbol and a "lion" the second symbol. Through numerous even several hundred of trips to the river, I discovered the secrets of these symbols. The River's Sky was different; it did not make one feel special. For the most part, it ignored you until it had a point it wished to make.

As I eluded to earlier, during the earliest years of my visits to the river nothing peculiar happened. I simply found a strong attraction and a serene comfort in just being there. Only after hundreds of visits did something strange actually take place before, it the River's Sky, audibly and verbally talked or should I say sternly admonished my deepest and most buried thought.

But twenty years before the strange things began the river was just place to go and fish. Fishing started early in my life, after listening to an old geezer I became quite the

fisherman.
I would later discover that as I went fishing to catch fish, the River's Sky had fishing plans of its own.

Chapter 29

But some experiences are esoteric, cryptic and filled with significant deliberate lessons through ordinary events.

The Detroit River at the foot of third would become my most cherished sanctuary. My oldest brother Stan, would always talk about going fishing. I had never been before. I knew only what I saw on TV. One day my mother took us to a park named Bell isle. This park was located quite a distance from where we lived. We would go there that day for our first time ever-family picnic. Stan was excited because he was going fishing. He would occasionally reach into his pocket to show off his bait. It was an earthworm that he had caught the night before. Several times he'd reach into his upper left shirt pocket, remove and dangle this dried up but still very much lively night crawler. Later after finally arriving at the park and locating a grill, he was permitted to go fishing on one of the islands shallow inland lakes, my mother was much to nervous to let all three of us go to the other side of the Island and fish the infamous Detroit River. So off he went, Stan fished and fished all day long. From afternoon till evening, reeling in and casting out, all day and we caught nothing. Absolutely nothing. As I recall. But boy was the whole thing fun.

Later as we got older, my mother would trust Stan to take us both Calvin and myself down to the Detroit River. The three of us would walk for what seemed like hours and no sooner had we arrived with fishing gear still in hand, when a car honked its horn had come to pick us up. We had just walked this long distance for nothing. But our momma was worried to death "I was worried to death" as she would put it of the idea that one of her three boys would fall into that big dangerous river and drown. But I had seen enough, I my affinity for the river had been made, I stood there that day for a brief moment feeling something, I liked this place, and there was a feeling about it I had never had before. It felt calm and welcomed. "Come on?" Stan yelled! I turn and ran to the waiting vehicle. My connection to the river would become vital, inseparable and all-important. Years would pass before my next visit but my next visit was sure.

As I got older fourteen or fifteen, my brothers and I sort of drifted apart. Each of us had our own group of friends and special interests. Calvin and I though would sometimes go on adventurous journeys together we'd walk everywhere. One of those excursions would take us back down to the river. Hey! Calvin said; let's go down to the river! Let's go down to the river and do a little fishing he said again, "Yeah, the river!" I began thinking; it's been a long time since I heard that suggestion, "let's go!" I said. After a quick plan of action, we were set to leave tomorrow morning at six o'clock, we were told that's when all the fish bite. This fishing thing Started with Stan, and for a while with Calvin but later would continue with me going it alone. By this age and time my mother was the least bit worried about us- our going to the river, because we had before then been to many places and had returned safely.

Later, I would make hundreds of trips to the river alone and she never worried. If she did she never showed it in her expressions. That day my brother and I made the long walk, it did not seem so bad, not bad at all, in a little time after crossing a few main streets, cutting across a few under construction freeways one was called Fisher Freeway, in the summer it would fill with water. Sometimes on our way to the river, we would make rafts from pallets left by the construction crew, separate into groups and battle each other by ramming into each other's raft. Of course it was dangerous, the water was pretty deep and their was no adult supervision the times we were there, but that's what fun was all about. After this adventure, we'd cross this landmark on our way to go fishing. These were long dangerous trips, crossing freeways, highways, railroad tracks, construction sites and man made rivers. Finally, we reach the old train station, this signaled we arrived at the river, "the foot of third" it was called.

It was a bustling place full of fishermen, and freight ships steaming down the rivers middle, seagulls squawking and flying overhead, people jockeying for the best fishing spots, some casting their rods way out, others just dropping them off the pier. Some fishermen were old others young, some stood others sat, like this one old guy we called "The old man and the contraption", this guy had some huge chrome gadget that he would set his rod (an ocean city it was called, very expensive, and very rich, after casting as far out as anything you ever wanted to see, he'd then place his rod in the contraption, place a large bell on its tip then sit, chat and wait. Then there was the Bob-Lo-Boats anchored right there at the foot of third. These huge turn of the century passenger boats were famous for taking people from Detroit to Bob-Lo Island amusement park over in Canada. I had never gone as a kid but other kids told me all about it. Some fishermen liked to cast just below these boats for feel they had better luck.

My brother and I baited our hooks then tossed our lines into the river along side other fishermen. We then waited and waited, occasionally reeling in our lines to check our bait. Waited and waited, still nothing. And just like my older brother many years before, we caught nothing. We would return at a later date and try our luck again.

This day we would arrive and as before bait our hooks and cast them far out as we could into the river, watch them drift way down almost parallel to the pier on which we stood. We picked a different spot this time though, it was a little further down away from the massive crowds. We fished nearly all day and caught nothing. To make matters worst so we thought it started to rain that afternoon. As the rain began, we along with all the other fisherman stood our ground. We carefully watched the ends of our rods for a nibble. The rain started to increase, the drops danced rapidly all over the surface of the river. Later as the rain got worse we along with other fishermen made a quick sprint for shelter. We chose an entrance way to the Cobo Hall Convention Center. From there we could at least keep an eye on our fishing gear. There was also a fisherman name Steve who was sharing the shelter with us. My brother and I were discussing our bad luck. We talked about the fact that we had fished all day and caught nothing, now to add to that was this rain. For us it seemed bad news all around for fishing.

Now Steve who we did not know at the time, was sitting or squatting with his back against the wall interrupted our private conversation and said, …"After a good rain the fish normally bite". This gave us hope and spawned more questions that required him to elaborate more of his fishing experience. One of the most important things, I remember it well, was how to bait the hook. "How did you bait your hook"? he asked, and in energetic animations I described how we took our big night crawlers and hooked it by the tail so that the fish seeing this will find it irresistible. Steve's eye's glanced to one side and back then he said, First, you break the crawler in half just below the saddle, might as well throw the head away or back into the can because its no good. Already I am in disbelief after hearing how to destroy a perfectly good night crawler. Does this old drunk even know what he's talking about? I recall thinking. Surely, a long dangling crawler is better at attracting hungry fish than a broken in half nub? Steve continued, after you're done breaking that crawler in two, take the lower half and slide it up over the entire hook so that none of the metal is showing. Leave just this much of the crawler protruding off the end of the hook (he demonstrated about an eight of an inch by hold up his thumb placed against the hook.) with this small-segmented tip of a crawler moving on the tip of a hook. This sure is not enticing to me if I was a fish I thought. Why if I where a fish I would would not even be able to see such a small piece of a crawler held practically motionless with only his tail showing and the rest of his body staked on a hook! "How long is your leader"? Steve asked, Leader? "You're going to have to make yourself a spreader with one leader extension." Well how long should this leader be I questioned? "About this long!" Steve demonstrated measuring a distance from the tip of his fingers to about his shoulder. "That long!!!" I replied. I was surprised because I had just purchased some fishing equipment from one of the best sporting good stores of the era, not just any sporting goods department store but the mother of all sporting good stores ZEPPS. They sold everything that a fisherman dreamed of, surely those sporting experts knew more than this old geezer, this old drunk! Why I could just see a fish on the end of that mile long leader line, you would never know you had a fish on the end of your line. He continued pressing the importance of this leader thing, “The longer the better” he said. How about this long I gestured with both my arms spread as far apart as I could get them, “No” about half that”. Again the length was about what he had shown me before. About as long as your right arm”. Give up my brand new double hitter spreader from ZPPS? I thought. I don’t know about this guy but he sure sounds like he knows what he’s talking about. But what really got my serious attention was when he said, you can be fishing along right next to Charlie China fisherman and beat him” he said softly, Charlie China fisherman I thought, wait a minute! Now I did not personally know this Charlie fellow but i would seen him several times. This was one of the guys walking the riverbank or dock with sometimes a load of fish dangling from each of his shoulders touching the ground. He also had a litany of hooks, spreaders, sinkers and spinners dangling from his cap, jacket lapel, and or boots. Along with the old man and the contraption, this was one of the legends that lived on the river. Beat Charlie china the fisherman! Yeap! He replied. Now I was in daydream land, I could just see myself going home with loads of fish, draping over both my shoulders. Man! “Looks like the rain stopped” This day it stopped some what abruptly, All right! I shouted and both me and by brother ran back out to the river dock to start fishing again.

I was very eager to test the new methods I had just learned from Steve. I quickly reached into my blue Cisco Lard can and pulled out one of the fattest night crawlers I had caught last night, reluctantly I broke him in half just below the saddle as instructed, impaired it on the hook, checked all my new spreader and leader configurations. Before I cast it out, Steve also had this thing exactly were and how to cast your rod. It was more like a toss than a overhead cast, "toss it to the left of where you're standing like this, he demonstrated. Even before that he checked the size of my sinker, it was too large and he suggested me switch to a small 2.5 oz lead weight. "Toss it to your left up against the current" he said. That way, as it sunk to the bottom, it would drift to land or settle right in front of you. "Don't cast way out"! He'd say. From that point it after the sinker drifted to settle just in front of me, I then had to lift and set lift and set the sinker a couple of time" stir up the mud", then let my rod settle at rest it on the pier and watch and wait.

I would wait and in just a few minutes, staring at the tip of my fishing rod as it lay on the pier, not upright but lying down, it suddenly jerked, excited I jumped and was immediately about to yank the rod, "wait, wait, wait" Steve standing near by and was quietly watching. My hand was under the rod, poised to snatch it up at the next movement, the tip jerked down again "wait…", there was a long pause then, the rod jerked downward two quick times "now"!, Steve shouted. I snatched the rod up off the ground and held it high; I could feel the fighting vigorously as the tip flickered forward and backward in rapid motion. I kept the string taunt as I began to reel and lower my rod at the same time. As the fish came close to the surface it fought even harder, I yanked it out of the water and it landed on the cement dock. The fish flipped and flopped all over the place. It was a big healthy fish called a perch. My first fish! I remember looking down at my first catch; it felt so good I was proud. This was a great moment for me, Steve's advice worked. I caught lots of fish that day, his system involved several techniques, each as important as the next, and none to be altered or omitted. At times I've varied the techniques some instances slightly and other times adversely, all with bad results. Over time I learned the importance of following instructions to the exactness as originally given. The man on the horse in the dream was unable to get my attention. He knew then that I would not follow anything to exact instructions as given. Be he did thrown me a lifeline. So I throw to you also, remember the DayStar. It became true that over time I could secretly out fish Charlie China fisherman, but hid my catch under water in a basket until such time I could retrieve it unnoticed.

My wife would be coerced to go fishing with me on a few occasions. On her first time out, I took her to one of my old fishing holes. I setup her tackle, spreader, sinker, leader, and spinner, baited the hook, and cast her rod into the river. Sure enough, she had the greatest streak of beginner's luck anyone there had seen. She out fished other anglers fishing right next to her. Soon as I mentioned to her, that it is time to leave, a couple of the fishermen immediately tossed their rods in her spot as I reeled her's in. One of the old fishing geezers traded one of his big sheep-head fish for several of her smaller tasty game fish. I Stranger Still:
agreed to the trade only because she was soooo excited over the larger fish, I kept most of the smaller fish—they make for better eating. Little did anyone know the secrets of the river were at work. The boy fishserman had covertly returned and being in firm league with the cloudHost, once again worked his magic, he he!

Chapter 30

From great distances, I hear…

"Each thing however seemingly insignificant and small is important as the next, as important as seconds to a day." I would hear these words clearly, as though a person was standing inside my mind. Each thing is connected, each is important. A seeming insignificant thing in one second can cause great calamity. A decision made in a split second, has infinite consequences.

As my older brother once said regarding chess, when one pawn move the whole board moves I thought. The voice would continue…certain individuals would need to be in control because one wrong act could affect the many.

The river was gradually imparting its mystery into my mind. What seemed an unlikely place to find a wisdom-quoting ally, Yes, ally! You must remember, even though externally I appear to have a normal life I was constantly in battle or should I say struggle with a hidden and much superior adversary, I did not know what I had indeed stumbled upon at the time. In a strange way, I was found comforted by seemingly insignificant words of wisdom. To me the river was just full of adventure. Yes, some strange things happened. However, in the very near future, the River's Sky, would become more to me in my struggles against "the boogieman"- secondMan than I ever imagined.

Chapter 31

There would be many days with me and this old river, I would go fishing hundreds of times alone and hundreds of times this place felt just like home. In a single day, I walked the river from the old Robin Hood Flour Mill to the Ambassador Bridge. Other days I watched the river, the sky, the rain, the clouds, sunrise, sun sets, the currents, the directions of the currents, the waves, the different types of waves, the fish.

One day I saw a big fish the water gradually darkens as he rose closer to the surface, gliding smoothly to his right side he looked right at me with a man's eye. He stayed on his side, he looked around, and he looked at my line, then back at me. Then slowly he re-submerged heading out in the direction of deep waters. It was as though I was face to face with another person not a fish. This was a fish but it had the brain of a person. Through his deliberate eye contact, he let me know that he knew things, that he knew me? The human minded fish then proceeded to conveyed the thought to that he was about to "head far out into deep waters", far out from the snuggled safeness of the rivers shore. I was left with the impression that he wanted me to prepare my life for a far away journey, prepare my mind for a far different life than the life I am now accustomed. Prepare to descend to the next level. I was left with the impression that my life was about to drastically change in some manner.

Chapter 32

Looking back later concluded that as I watched the sky, the sky was watching me. One morning as I stepped out onto the bank, I would be the first if not the only fisherman there. This spot was just east of "the foot of third" west of the old train station. I would like so many other times, i would set my spreader, sinker, bait my hook and then cast this new Ocean City, this was an all black fishing rod with silver stripes at each "eye" on the rod, very nice, it was for catching big fish. As I was saying, I would cast the rod as far out as I could. You would see a tiny sinker almost disappear and you would see a long arc of the silver cat cut fishing line as it created a trail of the sinkers flight reflecting a thin slither of occasional sunlight. The sinker should have landed far out into the river. That is not what happened that early morning "down by the river".

That morning when I cast my rod, the sinker flew out as usual; it would first go up then downward, only this time it never even slightly went downward. Instead, after it was cast out as far as it could go, it immediately went further, straight out as straight as someone had shot an arrow then climbed and climbed straight up to the sky! It was flying skyward, and then suddenly, so was I. I was being pulled up, pulled not floating, I know the difference between floating and being drawn by an invisible line from the sky, and this was not my fishing line, but an invisible connection that I could not see can feel. I did not panic. I was insistent on grabbing anything I could with my foot. I did manage to lock my right foot on a telephone barge and pull myself back down to grab hold, then further still nudging my body backward and backward gaining small ground, feeling the vibrations in the invisible line, I did manage to wrap this invisible cord around protruding dock pole protruding out the water. This maneuver took the strain off my body. I stood back looking amazed at what suddenly happened. To this day, I can still feel the vibration of the invisible current as I held onto the line. It was the exact; I said the exact same vibration I feel when the currents of the Detroit River flow pass my fishing line. Someone was communication to me. They did not use words they used symbolisms. They were telling me things. I would be alone many more days down at this old river with the River's Sky. After this incident, I could mentally detect the cloudHost found humor in my resourcefulness in maneuvers I took to prevent myself from being uncontrollably hauled up into the clouds.

The River's Sky is doing more than an ordinary sky. The sky at the river was not concerned about those other beings like my personal issues. It never discussed the adversities like the boogiemam. The River's Sky seemed more interested in better self-conduct, getting it right, paying attention to detail, "Are you awake" are you seeing? The sky would ask on occasion. Time will prove I was wrong. The obscure mystery behind River's Sky was more than I recognized. The meaning of the events would not manifest themselves until years later. River's Sky would prove itself more than just an unconcerned rude chastising enigma. It would prove to be much much more. The River's Sky did not treat me as some charity case. It reacted to me as though I was someone else, or as though I was an older mature and wise person who should know better?

All clouds are not as they seem. Clouds also are a symbol. I learned this symbol and can interpret its various forms. amnuitManreia(it is a host of many that move as one).

Chapter 33

I have witnessed the arrival of a small but powerful and great symbol. It arrived at the edge of our galaxy in the form of a falling star. I was permitted to witness the arrival of this one being whose name is Achieomene. At the same time, I was also permitted to see other entities who were also watching Achieomene make his descent outside earth's physical realm. The onlookers briefly communicated to my mind the circumstances surrounding this extraordinary event-taking place. The next morning I felt his mighty landing, thundering multiple descent spritatic layers. Debris and cosmic matter from his landing position sent debris flying over the horizon toward where I was standing. Earth experienced several days of mysterious, none stop rain. He was letting it be known to all that are capable of interpreting symbolism that he… has… arrived!

Sntcmetc himself, the great Moon, captain the rstanicamta host lost temporarily lost operation of his personal cloak during this unprecedented event. I could see his image, for the very first time! I could feel for the first time his emotion unabated, even though he is as a great moon of the night, I perceived his fear for the first time. He observed my watching and he knew I could see him. We watched one another. Slowly and ever so slowly so as not to cause suspicion and confirmation of what I was exactly witnessing, he slowly maneuvered the clouds in infinitesimal increments while gradually sliding behind them. With almost identical movement as the real moon would perform. However, I knew these were no ordinary clouds and this was not our moon. Remember, what I have told you about me and the feeling of matter, I feel and hear matter. Recall what I have told you of symbols, knowing what the symbol represent you know the being. This particular arrival of this FallingStar, is a threat to the host of secondMan also.

Remember I had said things could be best explained from the vanish point from the River? About the midpoint in my life and life experiences I understood much but much was still about to be learned.

I had begun to have suspicions that I was never alone. By this time in my life with all the experiences and encounters I thought I understood clearly what was expected of me. By that, I mean things like personal conduct do everything as instructed, never cross the line of misconduct, never get overly angry with my wife as I use to. Up to this point, you have heard about many things that happened to me. You would think that I in fact understood everything. You would even believe that by this time I believed everything that happened, I did, but not enough to "reflect". To reflect is to analyze one's experiences and adjust his direction. I've done that, so I thought, but what happened one morning would alter my life forever. If ever nothing caused me to reflect, this encounter involving another kind of over whelming presents would.

Chapter 34

One day my wife and I was in the kitchen, we lived in this house about twenty years. There was an argument over… I can not ever remember. After the argument I began thinking, I knew I should not argue or cause her even the minuteness of discomfort while I'm angry. In the household or in my presence, my wife must feel absolutely no fear or trepidations. I knew this! She could pout and sulk or have a tantrum and be one hundred percent wrong and I knew full well to do nothing but let her have her way, if she is a good wife, and she is. I knew this through observing them- the son's through their own eyes and from the many sermons of the far away orator. But I did not abide by this required law, to me it was miscellaneous, so during the argument I reached out and tried to hold my wife as she left the kitchen. She just moved her elbow slightly upward to avoid my grasp and headed for our bedroom still fusing at me. I did not make a second attempt to stop her. I did not even try to block her path. I use to remark that if other people heard what our arguments were about, they would just laugh. However, these were serious enough disagreements to us. That night we made up as usual because we did not believe in going to bed mad at one another. She fell asleep in my arms as with her head lying on my chest.

The next morning came and so did they, by the hundreds in full power from every direction. Now you must understand something, remember how I told you I have destroyed the sons of secondMan, his armies, and troops and have taken a third of his garrison? You would think I would be afraid of nothing, you would think that I would have mistook this invasion as a new attack from secondMan, I should have went into defensive mode and made a preemptive strike to take these intruders out.

And I would have, but these sons of Tenakkatonon of thirdMan are way different from they the RectnaHosts, secondMan. Also, this was my first face-to-face contact with them. They never had sat down and showed interest in my personal problems that I thought was important, just like the angry sky down at the river. I always thought there would come a time when something or someone would come and introduce themselves to me. And thinking back they did, long time ago when I was oh about fifteen still in Junior high school, still throwing bricks at rats at night. They appeared in a craft that silently stood about two phone poles in height, I know because I recall consciously estimating its size and height above the ground, and they said or someone from within the vessel said to my mind, "we control this", they moved a distant star to prove it then moved on. I guess this can be looked on as a hello, you know, like a welcome or something. But this, this incident that took place the following morning after our argument, the way they arrived, even more so for the reason, the reason they came as they did, carried a much deeper message. I am held to a higher standard. I did not know. I failed this requirement. I just did not know at the time. But now I know!

There I was lying in the bed fully woke early that morning, with my right arm around my wife as she lay on my chess like she often did even after one of our so called disagreements. Like I said this was a nothing argument by any definition. I was terrified at the mere arrival of the fleets. Zooming in from all directions, from the east, descending from the ceiling and bending gravity and matter as they landed sinking into the ground and then rising to re-align themselves to ground level. Hundreds of them, from the north, south, and from below they arrived coming, moving everything. I felt the same overwhelming power that day like the one years before in the apartment from the invisible wind that nearly blew me away. They materialized until my room and around my house were full. The commander's wide shoulders blocked my seeing some of them standing behind him. But, I could clearly see others standing with him on his right and left side. They all stood against the wall, my westward wall, looking at me. Not angry, just looking. But the biggest one, the leader, boy was he mad. He was very, very, very angry with me. He huffed and paced the floor back and forth for several minutes. He was furious. Looking directly at me, and very angry, I felt him say "you know you know better"! I dared not respond. I knew he referred to me upsetting my wife just the night before. After a while, he started talking through his still closed mouth to furious to open. Scowling me through his still closed mouth, for what I had done, done? All I did was touch her arm. I knew not to make any defense. Others nearby were letting me know whom they were, they are in control here "we control this!" As he continued, others started to move about the room. It was tight because it was full of them. Departure activity started, but this time there was no seeing the fleet of legions as they departed. No ground moving or any similar warp bending event that signaled their arrival. After the leader uttered his last of his muffled disciplined remarks they and he, all just vanished. Though I could no longer see any of them there was lots of activity still underway. Another being that was not initially present with the rest of the beings. He descended slowly over my bedroom ceiling he was saying lots of names, names of authority, names I've never heard before, and titles I could not understand nor remember. After this, he disappeared also.

I immediately shook my wife to waken her, I broke a silent code, I told her everything that had just happened. I somehow think they wanted me to do this, this one time. They wanted her to know that big brothers were in fact here!!!! So, unprecedented as the code of silence was, I knew to tell her and I did just that.

I concluded that a slight a deviation is not tolerated. I was on a stricter code of conduct than imaginable. You can notgo one step extra if you know you are not supposed to. There is no grace period to not do something. Nobody is going to want to tell you twice. What a welcome.

In reflection, I thought…they—this host, also had avoided my third senses all these years. Yet I can sense the movement of all matter seen and invisible, I feel the presence of the secondMan and the fleet, measure the span of his empires. All along, I had suspected being constantly monitored, I suspected that there was someone else, something else was here, but after this morning, all doubt was replaced with an even more strict code of conduct for me to adhere to. From this day forward, I took the sermons seriously. I would reflect on the incident, and not deviate ever again afterward.

I heard him preaching…
Be careful what you say or do, every action ripples the heart. Intensity of the ripples varies soul to soul.

Chapter 35

I visited the river more often after that incident.

While meditating at the river, the cloud hosts would notify me of their approach or presence, the waves on water would unexpectedly reverse direction. Then, looking up, a massive cloud host would appear and rapidly pour down coming to a fast stop just a few feet above the rivers surface. The trailing clouds extended far back over the skies of Canada in two opposite directions. It was my plan to sit at the river and meditate. It seem as though the cloud host sought to do the same, and it appear they wanted me in their presents.

I would conclude that certain things there is zero tolerance of Deep in my concisions knew I should not have caused my wife anguish that night. I should not have even lightly touched her elbow.

From great distances…

The weaker should not fear the stronger. If so, the stronger has weaker discipline. If the weaker insults the stronger, it is because the stronger has successfully concealed their true power.—*Tenakatonon Law of Host*

Again, I began to wonder… what am I, really.

Chapter 36

Enter the mMutota:

In Search Of AnioDomino - The mMutota Obsession

The mMutota has silently and covertly searched for sanwacharchtel for hundreds of years. The search has intensified over this time. The mMutota could never truly believe that a aniDiono could perish in the manner that sanwarcharcetel vanished. They were always suspicious because there was no evidence of disassembled matter in the area or zero-point he last occupied. In addition, the mMutota and other beings were aware of descent layer-nosus relocation. They and other highly advanced beings have recently perfected this relocation method allowing several light years of distances to be traveled in seconds.

To help solve the mystery of sanwarcharchetel's disappearance, several hundred million legions would be assigned to locate him. During this period, the mMutota sentinels scanned millions upon millions of minds on every specie and life form encountered. The examinations went undetected by other life forms living on lower descent-levels. Un-detection is possible as long as the mMutota conducts this operation from a higher level than where the hosts resides. They conducted with great caution an endless search on a cerebral level. Splinter groups engaged in all sorts of monitoring activities. They employed mMutota-controlled drone, android, and mind mists techniques. Scanning thousands of descent-levels, of which could occupy the same coordinates but very different and imperceptible realities. Any number descent-level could coexist right next to and simultaneously with others one unaware of the other.

This makes even a small space a large and arduous task for probing what amounts to a vastness of unimaginable scale. They, the mMutota-muucu scanned and probed relentlessly non-stop for several hundred years.

I did not know it at the time but in their search for fallenStar, many of us here had been scanned by the mMutota, me included.

Chapter 37

The incident I am about to describe took place over twenty-five years ago. There were times I could abruptly see these beings coming right up through the earth in their strange and silver machines. Some would briefly pause with their heads just above ground surface and do 360-degree scan, attach themselves to another approaching silver craft and continue skyward. At times there were many of them other times a few, they appeared unconcerned about us. It seemed they had other more urgent business to attend. I never did anything to attract their attention. I knew these sentinels were not my boogieman. One day an unexpected encounter with their commander hosts would take place.

Early one morning, as I sat in my daughter's room, I was accosted by several six to ten foot tall very muscular beings. In this instance, they were not in their silver ships, but did manifest themselves on a T-frequency – hiding themselves from those who see only physical white light. Their uniforms seemed to be part of their skin. They were reptilian like secondMan—the infamous boogieman but more human and looked much more physically powerful than any men I had seen before. This was definitely not secondMan. From nearest, I could tell or what they permitted to be revealed—I say reveal because I have learned that some beings control the science of mind sight, there were only seven of them. In addition, I did not receive the same threat from them as I had when encountering the boogiemen or secondMan. Although they never talked to me I could sense the thoughts in their minds. There was a deliberation of execution. Execution? Yes. Execution!

Sensing danger, I did know enough at the time to automatically run a mental mCryption routine on an automatic pre-accosted descent-level. This must be done in advance without obvious actions that would cause suspicion that an mCryption(mental dispersing of mind matter) is taken place. It must be done before any opposition forces are present. One must have control of his emotions and mental energies for one photscopic - emulation is itself a flare in the dark. The mMutota technology is of a mental matter nature, it involve sophisticated subatomic descent scanners, when I say scan I mean they inherit the mind, the history stored in the mind, even its subconscious thought record. My mCryption dispersing efforts were not good enough. Several more of them the beings, all of a sudden made their presents known from the darken shadows beyond the walls of the room and came closer to me, encircled me, a very powerful looking one emerged and walked very slow around my chair in which I sat. It was my daughter's chair, they had issued it in my mind, it then became physical matter and I sat as instructed. In one instant, I again moved information of various thought patterns from my mind on a subatomic level to atoms located about two feet in front of me inside the book storage area of the desk. But, at the same time this process would transfer my ingrams to many descent-levels millions of miles distance. Remember, this is subatomic mCryption, silent and unnoticed by any known detection method. The one being nearest to me, who circling my chair very slowly generated low thundering with each of his steps. I understood the symbolism of the thundering of the footsteps. This person was nothing to mess with. He circles the desk many times, as he walked ever so slowly. Wait a minute! Did he just detect my mCryption routine process? He actually acknowledged doing so by a slight tilt of his head and a quick glance of his eyes head focused on the very spot where I had dispersed the infinitesimally sub-micro ingrams. As he continued circling the desk despite his body movement, his head and eyes now remained focused on that spot. I could not believe that anything or anyone could challenge me at this point in my life. My level of fear became so high after realizing this thing could achieve what others cannot.

This silent interrogation went on for several intense nerve-wrecking minutes. I am embarrassed to even say, but this is the first and only time in my life I felt I had to go to the bathroom. Yes, I really felt that. I'm sharing that awkward moment as I share all the other experiences and events that surround the incidents, this way, you'll know I'm tell the truth at the expense of being embarrassed. The group summoned an image of my wife to my mind, she lay sleeping in the other room. Their consensus regarding me was concluded, I was being prepared for execution. I held back a sea of tears. These things were letting me have my last rights with the one they knew I loved.

Then the strangest thing began. All of a sudden, they abruptly conceded to depart. Just as calmly as they had arrived, they now deliberated that they must cease and go immediately. I still felt the consensus of execution even until they left by slowly fading themselves invisible as they started their descents.

The main interrogator, as he continued walking around the desk looking at "the spot" and in a strange way to send me confirmation making me aware that he is aware of the secret crypt ion process I sent.

I now know they, these beings were of the mMutota-macuu order. In reflection, they this particular life form was more different from any I had encountered to date. For one, they did not fear me. They did not find it necessary to paralyze me, as the boogieman had required. I thought them out of the ordinary and have reflected on them quite often over the years. They were too physically and emotionally different to be an off spring of secondMan. They seemed interested in searching for something else but unexpectedly stumbling upon me. In addition, I got the impression from them that somehow, I was far away, from where I was supposed to be. I was an enigma to them. I could read some of their thoughts as well. At any rate, they did not seem to be senseless murderers. I made myself believe that they looked on me as a possible threat and that is why they all of a sudden retreated. Later on in life I became more aware and I concluded that they considered me no threat at all. Perhaps they placed a higher value than I thought on the spouse wife relationship. I may be reading too much into this part, but it seems they made the connection after bringing my wife into the scene. Even though, I mentally detected them as extremely dangerous, much more than I was, but at the time, I did not rate them above secondMan. I was again wrong. Because in reflection, they did not have the same need to use any paralyzing fields before entering my presents. They knew what I was capable of and yet they did not even bother to immobilize or neutralize me. Yes, on second thought these beings were not afraid or threatened by my power. I later learn who they are. They are not abusive but do cause fear. I do not think they regarded the boogiemen a threat because they had to pass through that descent-level to reach my physical descent-level. I saw none of the boogiemen enter my descent-level for a long spell after the visit from the awesome strangers. However, the mMutota and I too would meet again in the very near future. Only this time I would know them by name.

Chapter 38

Humankind is faced with three hidden imminent evils; each event has the capacity to drastically alter the future of the human species.

The First Evil:
A powerful vortex is created at the arrival of the first fleet of seven armadas led by the famed and dreaded minanicta(undisputed commander of a thousand years) of the mMutota military arm. This commander visited me and deliberated my execution years earlier. Those on a physical level can mistake the arrival vortex as earthquakes and tornadoes.

Through my thirdeye, I have seen armies far greater than ours fall at the mMutota's arrival. I have seen the mMutota withstand the awesome firepower of the TolekAlwa. As the TolekAlwa were quick to scan and extrapolate that it was better to flee the advancing mMutota than risk any retaliation that can be afflicted on god knows what level of force the arriving mMutota pocessed. For even after the TolekAlwa unleased its massive arsenal, arsenal indeed, I understand semi-gammatic, subatomic disruption, matter disbursement and the like. The TolekAlwa has prevented invasion for many years. The TolekAlwa are well respected but are themselves aggressive in their pursuit for energy consumption and resources. They firepower is enough to devastated a solar system or family of small planets. You must comprehend the power of the TolekAlwa to understand the awesomeness of the mMutota. When the TolekAlwa own military detected the mMutota approaching on a T-frequency, they responded with sun like weaponry, three orbs of golden white-hot moon size fusion, enough force to split and disintegrate anything of normal matter within a light year radius. They employ crude, but gamma-splitting technology. Normally, this is enough and would rank you supreme if dealing only with physical beings or facing purely physical foes. The three massive orbs found their invisible mark but; instead of three large explosions, there was the sound of several soft thumps. No explosion, no flash of light, no ka-boom whatsoever. The TolekAlwa then unleashed a barrage of the same with the added conversion of what is best termed as bi-directional block blasts for several minutes… and nothing, nothing not even a flash of light from the mMutota garrison gliding overhead. It was as though they unleashed in mid air at a ghost of an enemy and not a real foe. Perplexed, all the TolekAlwa could now do was stand and stare. And stare they did, as they began to comprehend what was till that day incomprehensible. There is another life more powerful than their minds had imagined. There was no return fire from the mMutota, just a continuous arrival that eventually darken the skies overhead. Their massive arrival also caused the bending of light and the continuous altering of gravity fluctuations that caused the TolekAlwa populace to float sky ward. Machines, people and buildings, water, not all but many things went airborne. There was also a real danger of a threat if the mMutota decided to trans-pose into the telek's own physical dimension. This action might mark the end of the famed TolekAlwa and their solar system. To the telek the mMutota are more powerful and infinitely in number and vastness. They could take and absorb gammatic energy bi-directional firepower? What? Who is this mMutota? It seems they could arrival on a continuous basis for hundred of years. The TolekAlwa after several days quickly reasoned it was not worth having attracting the full attention of the mMutota-santacton(ruling body) and risk finding out the worse way what weaponry the mMutota themselves posses. So all-aggressive military action was ordered ceased and the TolekAlwa fled further into the distant stars.

The mMutota continued to arrive in earths region for months. The base of their vast ships appear as many odd shaped clouds as they cruise the galaxy and across the sky of galaxies. The arrival on one macto(one ship) can conquer galaxies by force. This ship also has zillions of sub ships that both pursue and lead, follow behind, and below the main mother ships.

The mMutota are always studying the environment in belief that many advances to their technology are attributed to replicating of things observed in nature. They will find nothing on this earth in man to emulate. Once they scan the minds of your many raping, wife abuses, child molestations, slavery, they will classify earth inhabitants as sub-human manimals (man-i-mal.)

Any specie that cannibalize upon itself are classified as be sub-human or manimal(being manlike in physical form but beastly in conduct.) Looking human, but are void of self-preservation. Most of us on earth have degraded to this murderous and apathetic state due to our sky brethren extracting moral igrams from our consciousness when we sleep. Even secondMan(known here as the boogieman) has not experienced murder by one of their own since their existence. This is a unique action inflicted only by earth bound humans on one another. This trait easily identifies earth humans as man-i-mal. Even their religion and law encourage them to war, murder and enslave against their fellow brethren without remorse. Earth maninals are the only one in the triad of human specie that engages in this conduct. They have no full soul or third eye sight, nor do they have anyone or anything as a guide to help them. What remains on earth is a by-product of manimals after years of bio extractions by secondMan.

Though the mMutota are evil by certain deeds, they possess not the gene of self-destruction, self-slavery and self murder. No such exploit can be found in their entire archive of collective consciousness. Any specie the mMutota encounter that cannibalize upon its own specie, might in threat of receiving the full rage of the mMutota.

If the mMutota do arrive and descend into physical descent-level of earth, we are doomed by their continous arrival alone.

However, this may not be the worst potential evil that the inhabitants of this cluster of star galaxies might have to face.

Chapter 39

The Second Evil:
A more immediate and threatening concern is hidden in plain view for over the past fifty years.

When my second function is called, you will see your most hideous murders suddenly for no visible reason, all of them at once, take to running as though they running for their lives. As they go a short distance, you will witness them all turn to a chromish metallic looking material, animating to bluish green hues, then shatter into a million dust like particles. This is a result of my second function being executed. To your most powerful of the military, down to the lowly street thug with murderous intent…you are already marked. The mystery of what I am and my purpose, is about to be revealed.

Function Call (A block of computer code that activates to perform a pre-defined function when its function name is called.)

What am I, really? The resident evil that live amongnst is about to find out. You will be as surprised as I was. What I share with you in this book in a couple of hours took me over fifty years of discovery.

In nearly every aspect, I have had an ordinary life. However slowly I have discovered late in life I am a A1function, a unit of the ArchimenusHost or known by his symbol – FallingSun. I'm a normal looking man but am in league with a concealed all-powerful military host that masquerade as clouds in the sky. I later realize that most of the many strange incidents since my childhood were not at all ordinary but intertwined with the live of other beings moving about but invisible to us and in some cases observing my consciousness and thoughts. The signs were always there but somehow evaded by all except my mother had some suspicions.

I started out and to this day remain a cordial and diplomatic person, in the present day however, I must execute two of my functions. It came as a slow shock to me, but I finally accepted what was happening in my life. I had what some old folk might refer to as a calling, a calling all right! A call to implement a eNetic(host-genetic time initiated function). This will pose a great dilemma for me, because to save humankind from detection by the mMutota I in one night must remove a evil percentage of mankind. In all my efforts, I am unable to resist executing this horrendous internal function and the time to initiate my function have been called. I write this book so that the good among you will not fear when you see evil being disseminated to dust.

Recall the story I shared earlier about my encounter with a saber-toothed symbol and the four janitors that stood by monitoring the confrontation. I was in fact being examined for courage, moral character and other conscious criteria. Do not inject your definition of janitor into this word. I too always loved house cleaning, gardening, especially the removing of all the weeds and vines that ravaged the garden if gone unchecked—this was something I did it with great satisfaction. I bring total extrication and am well prepared to cleanse the river of evil men and uproot the boogieman empire.

My first function is telling this story; it is the second function that troubles me. I too threaten to bring an evil to the earth. When a host function is called, it must execute. Bid me not a fault because it is not entirely my choice that I execute my functions, it is more the eNetic programming in my system. I have deep sentiment here, so before I act, I will explain. Remember, what I do, I do for the benefit of man at the expense of a few evil men. AclassFunctio-na(a code when called, interrupts the flow of evil to revitalize the waters.)

My second function, is to rid the earth of habitual genetically boogieman enhanced evil men. This will not be a hard thing to do, I have already told you of great battles and awesome wars that I have engaged with secondMan. I wished at times I could have inducted some of the most courageous men of earth with me but; they are not prepared to enter into another dimension-descent-level, with no physical weapons. Even a nuclear bomb is useless at point blank range against such adversaries as I have faced, and simultaneously maintain one's emotional delta and alpha levels while all hell breaks lose around you. I know among humankind there are no such men. Moreover, I have scanned the military generals myself and have found no mature men on this whole earth to help me against secondMan let alone the mMutota. To scan the evil and courageous, I employed a physical technique that involved sricaMit(set and retrieval of energy readings from micro-mites spread upon the human body.) Sounds strange? I have perfected many strange sciences far out of the realm of the normal physical discipline of physics.

My dilemma is that I must destroy some evil humans to save most of mankind, this in turn conflicts with my first and rudimentary underlying function…magnanimity which was one of the first words I learned by listening to the distant orator in the early years.

As I stated before, my second function you might find to be most appalling. Understand the options humankind is faced with and the mMutota I just described, it is either you deal with me or be discovered by the mMutota. In your present state of murder and sub-human behavior, the mMutota themselves will execute what they considered a favor to the universe; they will eliminate such a genetic cancer from further reproduction on a galactic and massive scale.

I very well maybe the second evil, but hear me out, hear all of what I say, see what my mind see and know why I must do a horrible thing to my own whom I once believed were

Chapter 40

To evil, I say be warned the mMutota is the least of your immediate concerns.

All these wars with the boogieman over the years, has changed my outlook on life. My attention turned toward resident evil that festers in our mist.

This year is more difficult than any other. In recent days, I've walked the floor many many times, from the family room, through the kitchen to the living room front door, there, I stare briefly out the small window and start the ritual all over again sometime for hours. I have also walked my favorite nature trail again this morning; this makes the second time in one day. This is one of the places I do my most serious contemplation. I use to circle the track only once or twice but all this summer I average eight to twelve times. It is about the meditation, the cleaning of the conscious, the preparing of the mind to perform an unprecedented action.

In my past as a youngster, out numbered twenty to one with no known weaponry at my disposal, courageously confronted gangs and criminals. I habitually did this in defense of the defenseless.

One day in my earlier development, while sensing the minds, I came upon an individual who had just physically inflicted a young girl. My immediate reaction was to immobilize him, and I did, he instantly fell to the ground paralyzed, I ran to the fallen man, I was getting ready to do further and perhaps fatal damage until an older woman standing by cried out in desperation "Son! Don't!" I ignored her. But her overly desperate plea continued. She said… "son don't! This is a house of God!" I froze, scanned the building and sure enough it was a church. I then transferred out of my defense mode and came to my conscious senses. I looked down at the woman, she was staring me eyeball to eyeball. I caught myself; I knew what I had done. I left the place walking down the street quickly. I felt ashamed sure, and even more sorrow for the emotions I had just caused the woman. I later learned from this first venture while mind sensing the importance and necessity of self-control, and that I just cannot habitually react to everything. What about the innocent bystanders? But today I'm fed up with what I sense, see, and hear. You will receive hundreds fold your terror. This is fourty years later and again, though more rational, I stand with the decision of attacking the most hideous of evils. Heed me, the old woman will not be here to spare you merciless murdering, killer of innocent, this time. Nevertheless, this is not easy. Though I hate evil, I have conviction.

Chapter 41

Occasionally my consciousness opens like a concentric circle, a ring of circles in water, expanding rapidly across the landscape, over a great distance. I feel the emotions of many crying mothers and neighbors and the joy of the murderer. I receive this emotion like ripple that come to shore. The minds of many crying persons I see and feel at night when my own mind explodes onto and then ride the tide of mental energy the mentalconntmca(that which binds all together and pass through mind matter.)

Do I continue to stand silent, as some great watcher as some impotent conscious reporter-like observer? Because I have the silver cord the conectedmta(the silver cord that connects our shared consciousness), I feel what others feel.

Many mornings I lay wide-awake with a heavy burden on my heart. I ask, do I sit idle by and let evil people murder the innocent? I ask my beloved mothers of evil children... do I sit idle and let your evil child kill another innocent? Because I understand motherhood, I also understand the mother of the evil and the mother of good. This is a hard thing, I know to place upon your mind, but as I said earlier, I myself am at a crossroad, bearing this heaviest of burden. I probably need your understanding or remission of what I am considering to execute upon mankind.

Do you for instance, consider the life of the evil of more value than that of the innocent? Alternatively, would you not eliminate the evil to spare the innocent?

Today I stand ready staring across the plains at an early sun rise this dreadful morning, thinking, and contemplating to cross another kind of plains if I can so say a mental plain of a heavy decisions that I've been pondering for the last several years but most recently for the past few months.

Soon, I will eliminate hundreds of thousands of the most hideous of evil men from the whole earth. Regardless of their proclaimed religious , be they rich or poor. There will be no eyewitnesses to my presents or actions. Therefore, in actuality I speak to the evil men with evil intent. For the good of your own loved ones postpone your evil thoughts and actions or suffer an unknown fate. To pure evil, those who delight is murdering of the innocent, rape of little girls, slave traders I say, by the likes of something you have never seen nor really wish to see, I know who you are and where you are, your pleasure in terror is coming to a most complete close.

Not one innocent will suffer, but many innocent hearts will be broken.

I am not sure what tomorrow will bring, how long I can hold out. At the tick of a clock, my conscious may be filled with an extension or urgency, I may be given the command to halt my action over night, and on the other hand, nothing may warn me or caution me by tomorrow. If so, this mark the end of evil and began a day of jubilee for some and sorrow for others

My head hangs low through out the day. I have found many positions to rest my head, placing it in my hands, in my palm, on the palm of my hand, both hands. Recently while walking through an office building a stranger yelled playfully at me, "get that head up, hold it up high!", I smiled realizing that my inner burden was manifesting outwardly. Her jousting was in fact a temporary lift.

Chapter 42

Perhaps it is time for evil to be the sacrificial lamb, if not voluntarily, then by force. If I am to prevent the near total destruction of us all, the good and the evil, I must sacrifice evil. For, the hate that it eliminates is like warmth from a glowing fire. Perhaps it is time for evil to be pruned, to be cut back; if this were true then I might accept my fate hesitantly and with reason. For I often wonder, if I came of these great powers by some greater will that provide and empower men as necessary in dire emergencies with what is needed for mankind to survive? Perhaps it is time for evil's exalted flame to be extinguished. Perhaps it is evils rightful turn to be sacrificed and inherit what it has sowed.

Chapter 43

The Third Evil: Then there is Achieomene.

I wish my commission to rid the world of pure physical human evil and the arrival of the mMutota were the only concerns, but there is one more. I had alluded to the arrival of this particular being in an earlier statement… the being named Achieomene!

At that time, I indicated that other entities were in attendance of the FallingStar. I also mentioned that they had communicated messages to my mind. Here is what transpired. They made me aware that Achieomene's arrival was not commissioned by the cloudHost. His departure from the host was one of his own volition—by his own free will. I also understood that his decision had to do with protecting another interest near earth's realm. This entity is willing to defend something of great value to him. During this time, I also mentally observed a second FallingStar trailing the first. This star did not emanate symbolisms of power. It followed the first star out of loyalty. Similarly, it also had great love for those it was leaving behind—the other entities that were watching this entire event and communicating thoughts to my mind. This event presents a unique dilemma. Achieomene has the potential to devastate this entire earth and the boogieman realm. What and whom is he protecting and willing to fight for? What might it be that will cause the ignition of his second function execute?

Any one of three aforementioned dooms day scenarios can devastate us all without malice. I cannot envision us avoiding all three, so I do warn… prepare yourselves.

Chapter 44

At this point, I can only tell you that life is not what it appears to be, life here is not what you have been taught. Most of what you've learned about earth is less than one percent of the whole truth.

We all are blind to certain realities, the river of man extends over vast amounts of time, and what appear to be boogiemen are in fact distant ancestors. What appears to be deity, again, are also distant genetic relatives. Of all three families of men, we are the only one in this vast link that is unaware of this primordial kinship.

In a matter of days our galaxy could possibly be encompassed and filled with unknown beings, they will seem to materialize from thin air.

As we the son's pass through the realm of secondMan's third descent-level where the most hideous loathsome of the boogiemen who have pilferage your minds at night for centuries reside. I will again execute my second function. At that time, you will hear thundering but see no storm, lightning but hear no thunder. What you will witness is the unleashing of strange Tenakatonon weaponry upon secondMan's empire in the hidden realm of the boogieman. For the first time the inhabitants of earth will see all six moons of earth.

Giant beings will fall from the invisible sky islands above creating large holes in the clouds as their bodies plummet down to earth. Your houses and buildings will fracture and rattle when they crash into the ground. The impact will echo and vibrate for miles. When you see the size of them, you will understand why all in the universe feared the boogieman for eons of time. If the trident that is carried by the one known as letractica of the boogieman outer realm falls to the earth with him, the size of it alone matches that of a large hundred foot tree. The ground will thunder at its impact.

If the mMutota transcend next to our adjacent descent-level, the initial mMutota arrival will generate friction forces that disturb molecules on the adjacent descent-levels. You will witness vast cloud formations. These formations reveal the outline of the mMutota crafts gliding overhead. If they seek to descent further into earth's physical space, the vortex of many tornadoes will follow.

Chapter 45

While writing this story I had to use complex cryptic methods every second of the day to conceal its contents.. They, the boogiemen will first see this story at the same time you read it. The boogieman sentinels are vigilant and know that something on an epic scale is taking place and they are ready to react at a moments notice.

Those things that have paralyzed you at night are not due to poor circulation. Those things are the legions of rectina, the boogieman or secondMan. They can see you, you can't see them. They often mock you nightly, and share your fantasies and replay your private experience (unknown to you while you lay sleeping) till they reach a drunken state then fall to the floor arms and legs sprawled out. Over fifty years I have seen watched them.

Chapter 46

By night fall as I sat to complete this story a erpto(smitus) rapidly approached my left side nervous and making me nervous he sat at the front of the couch looking out toward the window.

Later upon completion and leaving the room I turned out the light, I turned toward the window, I could see the partial rear of a giant size head that filled the picture window—a true guardian now stands closer and ever vigilant during recent nights.

Chapter 47

Over the past fifty years, my mind has experienced a most extraordinary voyage. Not so much in terms of great distances traveled; as it has been a slow journey of self-awareness and self-revelation.

A four hundred year epoch is about to end, at least on this side of the great river of man. To have a reality gradually unveil my personal mystery of my identity over a period of fifty years, many times I thought something was very wrong with my life.

Chapter 48

One of our last most admired, loyal and diplomatic igrams, will soon rejoin with the host.

After archieDomino's full recovery, we will have the capability ro drastically alter the course of earth's fate. One option would be for us to remain hidden and keep the mMutota on an endless quest, we could choose to return and destroy mMutota for they have no comprehension of our mutation that have taken over the years, or we could ascend to the sky and destroy the boogieman's empire.

Most of the cloudHosts stand ready intensely poised to leave this descent-level and head back home. A majority of the host piercingly stare far up the river, their minds on another place. We all painfully, yet patiently wait for the last ingram to become self-aware and rejoin the host. The intensity in which we wait is agonizing and will be matched by our speed in leaving.

unoDocomo—both my boots are encompassed by clouds.

I have rushed to you fifty years of secret hidden truths in one night.

Chapter 49

No matter where I go, no matter how far up the river on man, I will always consider this place, where I became self-aware and grew up, in the river of firstMan as home.

To any surviving boogiemen that have evaded the arrival of the mMutota or escaped our reprisal... I do warn, beware.

However, know for sure, when you hear the strangest kind of thunder after several weeks of uninterrupted rain, know that I did not rid the earth of all evil men. Know doom. Know that the mMutota has arrived.

To all that start to experience strange events after reading this story, to all that suddenly receive night visitations from invisible hostile beings entering your room in the middle of the night, in your darkest hour, in the darkest room,

with urgency I say…

"Remember the DayStar."

Other books:

ThirdSon and the River's Sky:
A series of seven short books that detail some of the dialog between ThirdSon and the mysterious River's Sky.

For other books that are available from this author, check this website at www.daystarbooks.com

DayStarBooks

www.daystarbooks.com

LaVergne, TN USA
10 September 2010
196686LV00004B/16/P

9 781452 864693